HORRiD HENRY'S
Merry Mischief

Francesca Simon spent her childhood on the beach
in California, and then went to Yale and Oxford
Universities to study medieval history and literature.
She now lives in London with her family. She has written
over 50 books and won the Children's Book of the Year
at the Galaxy British Book Awards for *Horrid Henry and
the Abominable Snowman*.

Tony Ross is one of the most popular and successful
of all children's illustrators, with almost 50 picture books
to his name. He has also produced line drawings for
many fiction titles, for authors such as David Walliams,
Enid Blyton, Astrid Lindgren and many more.

For a complete list of **Horrid Henry** titles
visit www.horridhenry.co.uk
or
www.orionchildrensbooks.co.uk

HORRiD HENRY'S
Merry Mischief

Francesca Simon

Illustrated by Tony Ross

Orion
Children's Books

ORION CHILDREN'S BOOKS
This collection first published in Great Britain in 2016 by
Hodder and Stoughton

1 3 5 7 9 10 8 6 4 2

A CIP catalogue record for this book
is available from the British Library.

ISBN 978 1 5101 0224 8

Printed and bound in Great Britain by Clays Ltd, St Ives plc

The paper and board used in this book are from well-managed forests
and other responsible sources.

Orion Children's Books
An imprint of
Hachette Children's Group
Part of Hodder and Stoughton
Carmelite House
50 Victoria Embankment
London EC4Y 0DZ

An Hachette UK Company
www.hachette.co.uk
www.hachettechildrens.co.uk
www.horridhenry.co.uk

CONTENTS

HORRiD HENRY'S THANK YOU LETTER

Ahh! This was the life! A sofa, a telly, a bag of crisps. Horrid Henry sighed happily.

'Henry!' shouted Mum from the kitchen. 'Are you watching TV?'

Henry blocked his ears. Nothing was going to interrupt his new favourite TV programme, *Terminator Gladiator*.

'Answer me, Henry!' shouted Mum. 'Have you written your Christmas thank you letters?'

'NO!' bellowed Henry.

'Why not?' screamed Mum.

'Because I haven't,' said Henry. 'I'm busy.' Couldn't she leave him alone for two seconds?

Mum marched into the room and switched off the TV.

'Hey!' said Henry. 'I'm watching *Terminator Gladiator.*'

'Too bad,' said Mum. 'I told you, no TV until you've written your thank you letters.'

'It's not fair!' wailed Henry.

'I've written all *my* thank you letters,' said Perfect Peter.

'Well done, Peter,' said Mum. 'Thank goodness *one* of my children has good manners.'

Peter smiled modestly. 'I always write mine the moment I unwrap a present. I'm a good boy, aren't I?'

'The best,' said Mum.

'Oh, shut up, Peter,' snarled Henry.

'Mum! Henry told me to shut up!' said
Peter.

'Stop being horrid, Henry. You will
write to Aunt Ruby, Great-Aunt Greta
and Grandma now.'

'Now?' moaned Henry. 'Can't I do
it later?'

'When's later?' said Dad.

'Later!' said Henry. Why wouldn't
they stop nagging him about those
stupid letters?

Horrid Henry hated writing thank you
letters. Why should he waste his precious
time saying thank you for presents? Time
he could be spending reading comics, or
watching TV. But no. He would barely
unwrap a present before Mum started
nagging. She even expected him to write
to Great-Aunt Greta and thank her for

the Baby Poopie Pants doll. Great Aunt-
Greta for one did not deserve a thank
you letter.

This year Aunt Ruby had sent
him a hideous lime green cardigan.

Why should he thank her for that? True,
Grandma had given him £15, which was
great. But then Mum had to spoil it by
making him write her a letter too. Henry
hated writing letters for nice presents
every bit as much as he hated writing
them for horrible ones.

'You have to write thank you letters,'
said Dad.

'But why?' said Henry.

'Because it's polite,' said Dad.

'Because people have spent time and money on you,' said Mum.

So what? thought Horrid Henry. Grown-ups had loads of time to do whatever they wanted. No one told them, stop watching TV and write a thank you letter. Oh no. They could do it whenever they felt like it. Or not even do it at all.

And adults had tons of money compared to him. Why shouldn't they spend it buying him presents?

'All you have to do is write one page,' said Dad. 'What's the big deal?'

Henry stared at him. Did Dad have no idea how long it would take him to write one whole page? Hours and hours and hours.

'You're the meanest, most horrible parents in the world and I hate you!'

shrieked Horrid Henry.

'Go to your room, Henry!' shouted Dad.

'And don't come down until you've written those letters,' shouted Mum. 'I am sick and tired of arguing about this.'

Horrid Henry stomped upstairs.

Well, no way was he writing any thank you letters. He'd rather starve. He'd rather die. He'd stay in his room for a month. A year. One day Mum and Dad would come up to check on him and all they'd find would be a few bones. Then they'd be sorry.

Actually, knowing them, they'd probably just moan about the mess. And

then Peter would be all happy because he'd get Henry's room and Henry's room was bigger.

Well, no way would he give them the satisfaction. All right, thought Horrid Henry. Dad said to write one page. Henry would write one page. In his biggest, most gigantic handwriting, Henry wrote:

Dear Aunt Ruby,
Thank you
for the
present.
Henry

That certainly filled a whole page, thought Horrid Henry.

Mum came into the room.

'Have you written your letters yet?'

'Yes,' lied Henry.

Mum glanced over his shoulder.

'Henry!' said Mum. 'That is not a proper thank you letter.'

'Yes it is,' snarled Henry. 'Dad said to write one page so I wrote one page.'

'Write five sentences,' said Mum.

Five sentences? Five whole sentences? It was completely impossible for anyone to write so much. His hand would fall off.

'That's way too much,' wailed Henry.

'No TV until you write your letters,' said Mum, leaving the room.

Horrid Henry stuck out his tongue. He had the meanest, most horrible parents in the world. When he was king any parent who even whispered the words 'thank you letter' would get fed to the crocodiles.

They wanted five sentences? He'd give them five sentences. Henry picked up his pencil and scrawled:

> Dear Aunt Ruby,
> No thank you for the horrible present. It is the worst present I have ever had.
> Anyway, didn't some old Roman say it was better to give than to receive? so in fact, you should be writing me a thank you letter.
> Henry
> P.S. Next time just send money.

There! Five whole sentences. Perfect, thought Horrid Henry. Mum said he had to write a five sentence thank you letter. She never said it had to be a *nice* thank you letter. Suddenly Henry felt quite cheerful. He folded the letter and popped it in the stamped envelope Mum had given him.

One down. Two to go.

In fact, Aunt Ruby's no thank you letter would do just fine for Great-Aunt Greta. He'd just substitute Great-Aunt Greta's name for Aunt Ruby's and copy the rest.

Bingo. Another letter was done.

Now, Grandma. She *had* sent money so he'd have to write something nice.

'Thank you for the money, blah blah blah, best present I've ever received, blah blah blah, next year send more money, £15 isn't very much, Ralph got £20 from *his* grandma, blah blah blah.'

What a waste, thought Horrid Henry as he signed it and put it in the envelope, to spend so much time on a letter, only to have to write the same old thing all over again next year.

And then suddenly Horrid Henry had a wonderful, spectacular idea. Why had he never thought of this before? He would be rich, rich, rich. 'There goes money-bags Henry,' kids would whisper enviously, as he swaggered down the street followed by Peter lugging a hundred videos for Henry to watch in his mansion on one of his twenty-eight giant TVs. Mum and Dad and Peter would be living in their hovel somewhere, and if they were very, very nice to him Henry *might* let them watch one of his smaller

TVs for fifteen minutes or so once a month.

Henry was going to start a business.

A business guaranteed to make him rich.

★

'Step right up, step right up,' said Horrid
Henry. He was wearing a sign saying:
HENRY'S THANK YOU LETTERS:
'Personal letters written just for you.'
A small crowd of children gathered
round him.

'I'll write all your thank you letters
for you,' said Henry. 'All you have to do
is to give me a stamped, addressed envelope
and tell me what present you got. I'll do
the rest.'

'How much for a thank you letter?'
asked Kung-Fu Kate.

'£1,' said Henry.

'No way,' said Greedy Graham.

'99p,' said Henry.

'Forget it,' said Lazy Linda.

'OK, 50p,' said Henry. 'And two for 75p.'

'Done,' said Linda.

Henry opened his notebook. 'And what were the presents?' he asked. Linda made a face. 'Handkerchiefs,' she spat. 'And a bookmark.'

'I can do a 'no thank you' letter,' said Henry. 'I'm very good at those.'

13

Linda considered. 'Tempting,' she said, 'but then mean Uncle John won't send something better next time.'

Business was brisk. Dave bought three. Ralph bought four 'no thank you's'. Even Moody Margaret bought one. Whoopee, thought Horrid Henry. His pockets were jingle-jangling with cash. Now all he had to do was to write seventeen letters. Henry tried not to think about that.

The moment he got home from school Henry went straight to his room. Right, to work, thought Henry. His heart sank as he looked at the blank pages. All those letters! He would be here for weeks. Why had he ever set up a letter-writing business?

But then Horrid Henry thought. True, he'd promised a personal letter but how would Linda's aunt ever find out that Margaret's granny had received the same one? She wouldn't! If he used the computer, it would be a cinch. And it would be a letter sent personally, thought Henry, because I am a person and I will personally print it out and send it. All he'd have to do was to write the names at the top and to sign them. Easy-peasy lemon squeezy.

Then again, all that signing. And writing all those names at the top. And separating the thank you letters from the no thank you ones.

Maybe there was a better way.

Horrid Henry sat down at the computer and typed:

Dear Sir or Madam,

That should cover everyone, thought Henry, and I won't have to write anyone's name.

Thank you /No thank you/ for the

a) wonderful

b) horrible

c) disgusting

present. I really loved it/hated it. In fact, it is the best present/worst present/I have ever received. I /played with it/broke it/ate it/spent it/threw it in the bin/straight away. Next time just send lots of money.

Best wishes/worst wishes/

Now, how to sign it? Aha, thought Henry.

Your friend or relative.

Perfect, thought Horrid Henry. Sir or Madam knows whether they deserve a thank you or a no thank you letter. Let them do some work for a change and tick the correct answers.

16

Print.

Print.

Print.

Out spewed seventeen letters. It only took a moment to stuff them in the envelopes. He'd pop the letters in the postbox on the way to school.

Had an easier way to become a millionaire ever been invented, thought Horrid Henry, as he turned on the telly?

✳

Ding dong.

It was two weeks after Henry set up 'Henry's Thank You Letters.'

Horrid Henry opened the door.

A group of Henry's customers stood there, waving pieces of paper and shouting.

'My granny sent the letter back and now I can't watch TV for a week,' wailed Moody Margaret.

17

'I'm grounded!' screamed Aerobic Al.

'I have to go swimming!' screamed
Lazy Linda.

'No sweets!' yelped Greedy Graham.

'No pocket money!' screamed Rude
Ralph.

'And it's all your fault!' they
shouted.

Horrid Henry glared at his angry
customers. He was outraged. After

all his hard work, *this* was the thanks
he got?

'Too bad!' said Horrid Henry as he
slammed the door. Honestly, there was
no pleasing some people.

'Henry,' said Mum. 'I just had the
strangest phone call from Aunt Ruby . . .'

HORRiD HENRY'S
BAD PRESENT

Ding dong.

'I'll get it!' shrieked Horrid Henry. He
jumped off the sofa, pushed past Peter,
ran to the door, and flung it open.

'Hi, Grandma,' said Horrid Henry.
He looked at her hopefully. Yes!
She was holding a huge carrier bag.
Something lumpy and bumpy bulged
inside. But not just any old something,
like knitting or a spare jumper.
Something big. Something ginormous.
That meant . . . that meant . . . yippee!

Horrid Henry loved it when Grandma visited, because she often brought him a present. Mum and Dad gave really boring presents, like socks and dictionaries and games like Virtual Classroom and Name that Vegetable.

Grandma gave really great presents, like fire engines with wailing sirens, shrieking zombies with flashing lights, and once, even the Snappy Zappy Critters that Mum and Dad had said he couldn't have even if he begged for a million years.

'Where's my present?' said Horrid
Henry, lunging for Grandma's bag.
'Gimme my present!'

'Don't be horrid, Henry,' said Mum,
grabbing him and holding him back.

'I'm not being horrid, I just want my
present,' said Henry, scowling. Why
should he wait a second longer when
it was obvious Grandma had some
fantastic gift for him?

'Hi, Grandma,' said Peter. 'You know
you don't need to bring *me* a present
when you come to visit. You're the
present.'

Horrid Henry's foot longed to kick
Peter into the next room.

'Wait till *after* you get your present,'
hissed his head.

'Good thinking,' said his foot.

'Thank you, Peter,' said Grandma.
'Now, have you been good boys?'

'I've been perfect,' said Peter. 'But Henry's been horrid.'

'Have not,' said Henry.

'Have too,' said Peter. 'Henry took all my crayons and melted them on the radiator.'

'That was an accident,' said Henry. 'How was I supposed to know they would melt? And next time get out of the hammock when you're told.'

'But it was my turn,' said Peter.

'Wasn't, you wormy worm toad–'

'Was, too!'

'Right,' said Grandma. She reached into the bag and pulled out two gigantic dinosaurs. One Tyrannosaurus Rex was purple, the other was green.

'RAAAAAAAA,' roared one dinosaur, rearing and bucking and stretching out his blood-red claws.

'FEED ME!' bellowed the other,

shaking his head and gnashing his teeth.

Horrid Henry's heart stopped. His jaw dropped. His mouth opened to speak, but no sound came out.

Two Tyrannosaur Dinosaur Roars! Only the greatest toy ever in the history of the universe! Everyone wanted one. How had Grandma found them? They'd been sold out for weeks. Moody Margaret would die of jealousy when she saw Henry's T-Rex and heard it roaring and bellowing and stomping around the garden.

25

'Wow,' said Horrid Henry.

'Wow,' said Perfect Peter.

Grandma smiled. 'Who wants the purple one, and who wants the green one?'

That was a thought. Which one should he choose? Which T-Rex was the best?

Horrid Henry looked at the purple dinosaur.

Hmmm, thought Henry, I do love the colour purple.

Perfect Peter looked at the purple dinosaur.

26

Hmmm, thought Peter, those claws
are a bit scary.

Horrid Henry looked at the green
dinosaur.

Oooh, thought Henry. I like those red
eyes.

Perfect Peter looked at the green
dinosaur.

Oooh, thought Peter, those eyes are
awfully red.

Horrid Henry sneaked a peek at Peter
to see which dinosaur *he* wanted.

Perfect Peter sneaked a peek at Henry
to see which dinosaur *he* wanted.

Then they pounced.

'I want the purple one,' said Henry, snatching it out of Grandma's hand. 'Purple rules.'

'*I* want the purple one,' said Peter.

'I said it first,' said Henry. He clutched the Tyrannosaurus tightly. How could he have hesitated for a moment? What was he thinking? The purple one was best. The green one was horrible. Who ever heard of a green T-Rex anyway?

Perfect Peter didn't know what to say. Henry *had* said it first. But the purple Tyrannosaurus was so obviously better than the green. Its teeth were pointier. Its scales were scalier. Its big clumpy feet were so much clumpier.

'I *thought* it first,' whimpered Peter.

Henry snorted. 'I thought it first, *and* I said it first. The purple one's mine,' he said. Just wait until he showed it to

the Purple Hand Gang. What a guard it
would make.

Perfect Peter looked at the purple
dinosaur.

Perfect Peter looked at the green
dinosaur.

Couldn't he be perfect and accept the
green one? The one Henry didn't want?

'But I'm obviously the best,' hissed
the purple T-Rex. 'Who'd want the
boring old green one? Bleccchhhh.'

'It's true, I'm not as good as the
purple one,' sobbed the green dinosaur.
'The purple is for big boys, the green is
for babies.'

'I want the purple one!' wailed Peter. He started to cry.

'But they're exactly the same,' said Mum. 'They're just different colours.'

'I want the purple one!' screamed Henry and Peter.

'Oh dear,' said Grandma.

'Henry, you're the eldest, let Peter have the purple one,' said Dad.

WHAT?

'NO!' said Horrid Henry. 'It's mine.' He clutched it tightly.

'He's only little,' said Mum.

'So?' said Horrid Henry. 'It's not fair. I want the purple one!'

'Give it to him, Henry,' said Dad.

'NOOOOOOO!' screamed Henry. 'NOOOOOOO!'

'I'm counting, Henry,' said Mum. 'No TV tonight . . . no TV tomorrow . . . no TV . . .'

'NOOOO!' screamed Horrid Henry.
Then he hurled the purple dinosaur at
Peter.

Henry could hardly believe what had
just happened. Just because he was the
oldest, he had to take the bad present?
It was totally and utterly and completely
unfair.

'I want the purple one!'

'You know that "I want doesn't get",'
said Peter. 'Isn't that right, Mum?'

'It certainly is,' said Mum.

Horrid Henry pounced. He was a ginormous crocodile chomping on a very chewy child.

'AAAIIIEEEEE!' screamed Peter. 'Henry bit me.'

'Don't be horrid, Henry!' shouted Mum. 'Poor Peter.'

'Serves him right!' shrieked Horrid Henry. 'You're the meanest parents in the world and I hate you.'

'Go to your room!' shouted Dad.

'No pocket money for a week!' shouted Mum.

'Fine!' screamed Horrid Henry.

Horrid Henry sat in his bedroom.
He glared at the snot-green dinosaur
scowling at him from where he'd
thrown it on the floor and stomped on
it. He hated the colour green. He loved

the colour purple. The leader of the
Purple Hand Gang deserved the purple
Dinosaur Roar.

He'd make Peter swap dinosaurs if it
was the last thing he did. And if Peter
wouldn't swap, he'd be sorry he was
born. Henry would . . . Henry could . . .

And then suddenly Horrid Henry had a wonderful, wicked idea. Why had he never thought of this before?

✳

Perfect Peter sat in his bedroom. He smiled at the purple dinosaur as it lurched roaring around the room.

'RRRRAAAAAAAAA! RAAAAAAAAA! FEED ME!' bellowed the dinosaur.

How lucky he was to have the purple dinosaur. Purple was much better than green. It was only fair that Peter got the purple dinosaur, and Henry got the yucky green one. After all, Peter was perfect and Henry was horrid. Peter deserved the purple one.

Suddenly Horrid Henry burst into his bedroom.

'Mum said to stay in your room,' squealed Peter, shoving the dinosaur under his desk and standing guard in front of it. Henry would have to drag him away kicking and screaming before he got his hands on Peter's T-Rex.

'So?' said Henry.

'I'm telling on you,' said Peter.

'Go ahead,' said Henry. 'I'm telling on *you*, wibble pants.'

Tell on him? Tell what?

'There's nothing to tell,' said Perfect Peter.

'Oh yes there is,' said Henry. 'I'm going to tell everyone what a mean horrid wormy toad you are, stealing the purple dinosaur when I said I wanted it first.'

Perfect Peter gasped. Horrid? Him?

'I didn't steal it,' said Peter. 'And I'm not horrid.'

'Are too.'

'Am not. I'm perfect.'

'No you're not. If you were *really* perfect, you wouldn't be so selfish,' said Henry.

'I'm not selfish,' whimpered Peter.

But *was* he being selfish keeping the purple dinosaur, when Henry wanted it so badly?

'Mum and Dad said I could have it,' said Peter weakly.

'That's 'cause they knew you'd just start crying,' said Henry. 'Actually,

they're disappointed in you. I heard
them.'

'What did they say?' gasped Peter.

'That you were a crybaby,' said
Henry.

'I'm not a crybaby,' said Peter.

'Then why are you acting like one,
crybaby?'

Could Henry be telling the truth?
Mum and Dad . . . disappointed in him
. . . thinking he was a baby? A selfish
baby? A *horrid* selfish baby?

Oh no, thought Peter. Could Henry
be right? *Was* he being horrid?

'Go on, Peter,' urged his angel. 'Give
Henry the purple one. After all, they're
exactly the same, just different colours.'

'Don't do it!' urged his devil.
'Why should you always be perfect? Be
horrid for once.'

'Uhmm, uhmm,' said Peter.

'You know you want to do the right thing,' said Henry.

Peter did want to do the right thing.

'Okay, Henry,' said Peter. 'You can have the purple dinosaur. I'll have the green one.'

YES!!!

Slowly Perfect Peter crawled under his desk and picked up the purple dinosaur.

'Good boy, Peter,' said his angel.

'Idiot,' said his devil.

Slowly Peter held out the dinosaur to Henry. Henry grabbed it . . .

Wait. Was he crazy? Why should
he swap with Henry? Henry was only
trying to trick him . . .

'Give it back!' yelled Peter.

'No!' said Henry.

Peter tugged on the dinosaur's legs.

Henry tugged on the dinosaur's head.

'Gimme!'

'Gimme!'

Tug
Tug
Yank
Yank
Snaaaaap.
Riiiiiiip.

Horrid Henry looked at the twisted
purple dinosaur head in his hands.

Perfect Peter looked at the broken
purple dinosaur claw in his hands.

'I want the green dinosaur!' shrieked
Henry and Peter.

HORRID HENRY
EATS A VEGETABLE

'Ugggh! Gross! Yuck! Bleeeeeech!'

Horrid Henry glared at the horrible,
disgusting food slithering on his plate.
Globby slobby blobs. Bumpy lumps.
Rubbery blubbery globules of glop.
Ugghh!

How Dad and Mum and Peter could
eat this swill without throwing up was
amazing. Henry poked at the white,
knobbly clump. It looked like brains.
It felt like brains. Maybe it was . . .
Ewwwwwww.

Horrid Henry pushed away his plate.

'I can't eat this,' moaned Henry. 'I'll be sick!'

'Henry! Cauliflower cheese is delicious,' said Mum.

'And nutritious,' said Dad.

'I love it,' said Perfect Peter. 'Can I have seconds?'

'It's nice to know *someone* appreciates my cooking,' said Dad. He frowned at Henry.

'But I hate vegetables,' said Henry. Yuck. Vegetables were so . . . healthy. And tasted so . . . vegetably. 'I want pizza!'

'Well, you can't have it,' said Dad.

'Ralph has pizza and chips every night at his house,' said Henry. 'And Graham never has to eat vegetables.'

'I don't care what Ralph and Graham eat,' said Mum.

'You've got to eat more vegetables,' said Dad.

'I eat loads of vegetables,' said Henry.

'Name one,' said Dad.

'Crisps,' said Henry.

'Crisps aren't vegetables, are they, Mum?' said Perfect Peter.

'No,' said Mum. 'Go on, Henry.'

'Ketchup,' said Henry.

'Ketchup is not a vegetable,' said Dad.

'It's impossible cooking for you,' said Mum.

'You're such a picky eater,' said Dad.

'I eat loads of things,' said Henry.

'Like what?' said Dad.

'Chips. Crisps. Burgers. Pizza. Chocolate. Sweets. Cake. Biscuits. Loads of food,' said Horrid Henry.

'That's not very healthy, Henry,' said Perfect Peter. 'You haven't said any fruit or vegetables.'

'So?' said Henry. 'Mind your own business, Toad.'

'Henry called me Toad,' wailed Peter.

'Ribbet. Ribbet,' croaked Horrid Henry.

'Don't be horrid, Henry,' snapped Dad.

'You can't go on eating so unhealthily,' said Mum.

'Agreed,' said Dad.

Uh oh, thought Henry. Here it comes. Nag nag nag. If there were

prizes for best naggers Mum and Dad
would win every time.

'I'll make a deal with you, Henry,'
said Mum.

'What?' said Henry suspiciously. Mum
and Dad's 'deals' usually involved his
doing something horrible, for a pathetic
reward. Well no way was he falling for
that again.

'If you eat all your vegetables for
five nights in a row, we'll take you to
Gobble and Go.'

Henry's heart missed a beat. Gobble
and Go! Gobble and Go! Only Henry's
favourite restaurant in the whole wide
world. Their motto: 'The chips just
keep on coming!' shone forth from a
purple neon sign. Music blared from
twenty loudspeakers. Each table had its
own TV. You could watch the chefs
heat up your food in a giant microwave.

Best of all, grown-ups never wanted to hang about for hours and chat. You ordered, gobbled, and left. Heaven.

And what fantastic food! Jumbo burgers. Huge pizzas. Lakes of ketchup. As many chips as you could eat. Fifty-two different ice creams. And not a vegetable in sight.

For some reason Mum and Dad hated Gobble and Go. They'd taken him once, and sworn they would never go again.

And now, unbelievably, Mum was offering.

'Deal!' shouted Henry, in case she changed her mind.

'So we're agreed,' said Mum. 'You eat your vegetables every night for five nights, and then we'll go.'

'Sure. Whatever,' said Horrid Henry eagerly. He'd agree to anything for a

meal at Gobble and Go. He'd agree to
dance naked down the street singing
'Hallelujah! I'm a nudie!' for the chance
to eat at Gobble and Go.

Perfect Peter stopped eating his
cauliflower. He didn't look very happy.

'I always eat *my* vegetables,' said Peter.
'What's my reward?'

'Health,' said Mum.

*

Day 1. String beans.

'Mum, Henry hasn't eaten any beans
yet,' said Peter.

'I have too,' lied Henry.

'No you haven't,' said Peter. 'I've been watching.'

'Shut up, Peter,' said Henry.

'Mum!' wailed Peter. 'Henry told me to shut up.'

'Don't tell your brother to shut up,' said Mum.

'It's rude,' said Dad. 'Now eat your veg.'

Horrid Henry glared at his plate, teeming with slimy string beans. Just like a bunch of green worms, he thought. Yuck.

He must have been mad agreeing to eat vegetables for five nights in a row. He'd be poisoned before day three. Then they'd be sorry. 'How could we have been so cruel?' Mum

would shriek. 'We've killed our own son,' Dad would moan. 'Why oh why did we make him eat his greens?' they would sob.

Too bad he'd be dead so he couldn't scream, 'I told you so!'

'We have a deal, Henry,' said Dad.

'I know,' snapped Henry.

He cut off the teeniest, tiniest bit of string bean he could.

'Go on,' said Mum.

Slowly, Horrid Henry lifted his fork and put the poison in his mouth.

Aaaarrrgggghhhhhh! What a horrible taste! Henry spat and spluttered as the sickening sliver of string bean stuck in his throat.

'Water!' he gasped.

Perfect Peter speared several beans and popped them in his mouth.

'Great string beans, Dad,' said Peter.

'So crispy and crunchy.'

'Have mine if you like them so much,' muttered Henry.

'I want to see you eat every one of those string beans,' said Dad. 'Or no Gobble and Go.'

Horrid Henry scowled. No way was he eating another mouthful. The taste was too horrible. But, oh, Gobble and Go. Those burgers! Those chips! Those TVs!

There had to be another way. Surely he, King Henry the Horrible, could defeat a plate of greens?

51

Horrid Henry worked out his battle plan. It was dangerous. It was risky. But what choice did he have?

First, he had to distract the enemy.

'You know, Mum,' said Henry, pretending to chew, 'you were right. These beans are very tasty.'

Mum beamed.

Dad beamed.

'I told you you'd like them if you tried them,' said Mum.

Henry pretended to swallow, then speared another bean. He pushed it round his plate.

Mum got up to refill the water jug. Dad turned to speak to her. Now was his chance!

Horrid Henry stretched out his foot under the table and lightly tickled Peter's leg.

'Look out, Peter, there's a spider on

your leg.'

'Where?' squealed Peter, looking
frantically under the table.

Leap! Plop!

Henry's beans hopped onto Peter's
plate.

Peter raised his head.

'I don't see any spider,' said Peter.

'I knocked it off,' mumbled Henry,
pretending to chew vigorously.

Then Peter saw his plate, piled high
with string beans.

'Ooh,' said Peter, 'lucky me! I thought I'd finished!'

Tee hee, thought Horrid Henry.

✳

Day 2. Broccoli.

Plip!

A piece of Henry's broccoli 'accidentally' fell on the floor. Henry kicked it under Peter's chair.

Plop! Another piece of Henry's broccoli fell. And another. And another.

Plip plop. Plip plop. Plip plop.

Soon the floor under Peter's chair was littered with broccoli bits.

'Mum!' said Henry. 'Peter's making a mess.'

'Don't be a telltale, Henry,' said Dad.

'He's always telling on *me*,' said Henry.

Dad checked under Peter's chair.

'Peter! Eat more carefully. You're not

a baby any more.'

Ha ha ha thought Horrid Henry.

✱

Day 3. Peas.

Squish!

Henry flattened a pea under his knife.

Squash!

Henry flattened another one.

Squish. Squash. Squish.

Squash.

Soon every
pea was safely
squished and

hidden under Henry's knife.

'Great dinner, Dad,' said Horrid
Henry. 'Especially the peas. I'll clear,'
he added, carrying his plate to the sink
and quickly rinsing his knife.

Dad beamed.

'Eating vegetables is making you
helpful,' said Dad.

'Yes,' said Henry sweetly. 'It's great being helpful.'

✱

Day 4. Cabbage.

Buzz.

Buzz.

'A fly landed on my cabbage!' shrieked Henry. He swatted the air with his hands.

'Where?' said Mum.

'There!' said Henry. He leapt out of his seat. 'Now it's on the fridge!'

'Buzz,' said Henry under his breath.

'I don't see any fly,' said Dad.

'Up there!' said Henry, pointing to the ceiling.

Mum looked up.

Dad looked up.

Peter looked up.

Henry dumped a handful of cabbage in the bin. Then he sat back down at the table.

'Rats,' said Henry. 'I can't eat the rest of my cabbage now, can I? Not after a filthy horrible disgusting fly has walked all over it, spreading germs and dirt and poo and—'

'All right all right,' said Dad. 'Leave the rest.'

I am a genius, thought Horrid Henry, smirking. Only one more battle until – Vegetable Victory!

✳

Day 5. Sprouts.

Mum ate her sprouts.

Dad ate his sprouts.

57

Peter ate his sprouts.

Henry glared at his sprouts. Of all the miserable, rotten vegetables ever invented, sprouts were the worst. So bitter. So stomach-churning. So . . . green.

But how to get rid of them? There was Peter's head, a tempting target. A very tempting target. Henry's sprout-flicking fingers itched. No, thought Horrid Henry. I can't blow it when I'm so close.

Should he throw them on the floor? Spit them in his napkin?

Or – Horrid Henry beamed.

There was a little drawer in the table in front of Henry's chair. A perfect, brussel sprout-sized drawer.

Henry eased it open. What could be simpler than stuffing a sprout or two inside while pretending to eat?

Soon the drawer was full. Henry's plate was empty.

'Look Mum! Look Dad!' screeched Henry. 'All gone!' Which was true, he thought gleefully.

'Well done, Henry,' said Dad.

'Well done, Henry,' said Peter.

'We'll take you to Gobble and Go tomorrow,' said Mum.

'Yippee!' screamed Horrid Henry.

✷

Mum, Dad, Henry, and Peter walked up the street.

Mum, Dad, Henry, and Peter walked down the street.

Where was Gobble and Go, with its flashing neon sign, blaring music, and purple walls? They must have walked past it.

But how? Horrid Henry looked about wildly. It was impossible to miss Gobble

and Go. You could see that neon sign
for miles.

'It was right here,' said Horrid Henry.
But Gobble and Go was gone.

A new restaurant squatted in its place.

'The Virtuous Veggie,' read the sign.
'The all new, vegetable restaurant!'

Horrid Henry gazed in horror at the
menu posted outside.

'Yummy!' said Perfect Peter.

Cabbage Casserole
Pop-up Peas
Spinach Surprise
Sprouts a go-go
Choice of rhubarb or
broccoli ice cream

'Look, Henry,' said Mum. 'It's serving all your new favourite vegetables.'

Horrid Henry opened his mouth to protest. Then he closed it. He knew when he was beaten.

HORRiD HENRY'S RAINY DAY

Horrid Henry was bored. Horrid Henry
was fed up. He'd been banned from the
computer for rampaging through Our
Town Museum. He'd been banned
from watching TV just because he was
caught watching a *teeny* tiny bit extra
after he'd been told to switch it off
straight after *Mutant Max*. Could he
help it if an exciting new series about
a rebel robot had started right after?
How would he know if it was any good
unless he watched some of it?

It was completely unfair and all Peter's
fault for telling on him, and Mum and
Dad were the meanest, most horrible
parents in the world.

And now he was stuck indoors, all day
long, with absolutely nothing to do.

The rain splattered down. The house
was grey. The world was grey. The
universe was grey.

'I'm bored!' wailed Horrid Henry.

'Read a book,' said Mum.

'Do your homework,' said Dad.

'NO!' said Horrid Henry.

'Then tidy your room,' said Mum.

'Unload the dishwasher,' said Dad.

'Empty the bins,' said Mum.

'NO WAY!' shrieked Horrid Henry. What was he, a slave? Better keep out of his parents' way, or they'd come up with even more horrible things for him to do.

Horrid Henry stomped up to his boring bedroom and slammed the door. Uggh. He hated all his toys. He hated all his music. He hated all his games.

UGGGHHHHHH! What could he do?

Aha.

He could always check to see what Peter was up to.

Perfect Peter was sitting in his room arranging stamps in his stamp album.

'Peter is a baby, Peter is a baby,'

jeered Horrid Henry, sticking his head
round the door.

'Don't call me baby,' said Perfect
Peter.

'OK, Duke of Poop,' said Henry.

'Don't call me Duke!' shrieked Peter.

'OK, Poopsicle,' said Henry.

'MUUUUM!' wailed Peter. 'Henry
called me Poopsicle!'

'Don't be horrid, Henry!' shouted
Mum. 'Stop calling your brother names.'

Horrid Henry smiled sweetly at Peter.

'OK, Peter, 'cause I'm so nice, I'll let you make a list of ten names that you don't want to be called,' said Henry. 'And it will only cost you £1.'

£1! Perfect Peter could not believe his ears. Peter would pay much more than that never to be called Poopsicle again.

'Is this a trick, Henry?' said Peter.

'No,' said Henry. 'How dare you? I make you a good offer, and you accuse me. Well, just for that—'

'Wait,' said Peter. 'I accept.' He handed Henry a pound coin. At last, all those horrid names would be banned. Henry would never call him Duke of Poop again.

Peter got out a piece of paper and a pencil.

Now, let's see, what to put on the list, thought Peter. Poopsicle, for a

67

start. And I hate being called Baby, and Nappy Face, and Duke of Poop. Peter wrote and wrote and wrote.

'OK, Henry, here's the list,' said Peter.

NAMES I DON'T WANT TO BE CALLED

1. Poopsicle
2. Duke of Poop
3. Ugly
4. Nappy face
5. Baby
6 Toad
7. Smelly toad
8. Ugg
9. Worm
10. Wibble pants

Horrid Henry scanned the list. 'Fine, pongy pants,' said Henry. 'Sorry, I meant poopy pants. Or was it smelly nappy?'

'MUUUMM!' wailed Peter. 'Henry's calling me names!'

'Henry!' screamed Mum. 'For the last time, can't you leave your brother alone?'

Horrid Henry considered. *Could* he leave that worm alone?

'Peter is a frog, Peter is a frog,' chanted Henry.

'MUUUUUUMMMMM!' screamed Peter.

'That's it, Henry!' shouted Mum. 'No pocket money for a week. Go to your room and stay there.'

'Fine!' shrieked Henry. 'You'll all be sorry when I'm dead.' He stomped

down the hall and slammed his bedroom
door as hard as he could. *Why* were his
parents so mean and horrible? He was
hardly bothering Peter at all. Peter *was*
a frog. Henry was only telling the
truth.

Boy would they be sorry when he'd
died of boredom stuck up here.

If only we'd let him
watch a little extra TV,
Mum would wail. Would
that have been so terrible?

If only
we hadn't
made him do any chores,
Dad would sob.

Why didn't
I let Henry
call me names, Peter
would howl. After all,
I do have smelly pants.

And now it's too late and we're soooooooo sorry, they would shriek.

But wait. *Would* they be sorry? Peter would grab his room. And all his best toys. His arch enemy Stuck-Up Steve could come over and snatch anything he wanted, even his skeleton bank and Goo-Shooter. Peter could invade the Purple Hand fort and Henry couldn't stop him. Moody Margaret could hop over the wall and nick his flag. And his biscuits. And his Dungeon Drink Kit. Even his . . . Supersoaker.

NOOOOOO!!!

Horrid Henry went pale. He had to stop those rapacious thieves. But how?

I could come back and haunt them, thought Horrid Henry. Yes! That would teach those grave-robbers not to mess with me.

'OOOOOOO, get out of my rooooooooooom, you horrrrrrrible toooooooooooad,' he would moan at Peter.

'Touch my Goooooooo-shoooooter and you'll be morphed into ectoplasm,' he'd groan spookily from under Stuck-Up Steve's bed. Ha! That would show him.

Or he'd pop out from inside Moody Margaret's wardrobe.

'Giiiiive Henrrrrry's toyyyys back, you mis-er-a-ble sliiiiiimy snake,' he would rasp. That would teach her a thing or two.

Henry smiled. But fun as it would
be to haunt people, he'd rather stop
horrible enemies snatching his stuff in
the first place.

And then suddenly Horrid Henry had
a brilliant, spectacular idea. Hadn't Mum
told him just the other day that people
wrote wills to say who they wanted to
get all their stuff when they died? Henry
had been thrilled.

'So when you die I get all your money!' Henry beamed.  Wow. The house would be his! And the car! And he'd be boss of the TV, 'cause it would be his, too!!! And the only shame was—

'Couldn't you just give it all to me now?' asked Henry.

'Henry!' snapped Mum. 'Don't be horrid.'

There was no time to lose. He had to write a will immediately.

Horrid Henry sat down at his desk and grabbed some paper.

MY WILL
WARNING: DO NOT READ UNLESS
I AM DEAD!!!! I mean it!!!!

If you're reading this it's because I'm dead and you aren't. I wish you were dead and I wasn't, so I could have all your stuff. It's so not fair.

First of all, to anyone thinking of snatching my stuff just 'cause I'm dead . . . BEWARE! Anyone who doesn't do what I say will get haunted by a bloodless and boneless ghoul, namely me. So there.

Now the hard bit, thought Horrid Henry. Who should get his things? Was anyone deserving enough?

Peter, you are a worm. And a toad. And an ugly baby nappy face smelly ugg wibble pants poopsicle. I leave you . . . hmmmn. That toad really shouldn't get anything. But Peter was his brother after all. **I leave you my sweet wrappers. And a muddy twig.**

That was more
than Peter deserved.
Still . . .

Steve, you are stuck-up and horrible and the world's worst cousin. You can have a pair of my socks. You can choose the blue  ones with the holes or the falling down orange ones.

Margaret, you nit-face. I give you the Purple Hand flag to remember me by—NOT!

You can have two radishes and the knight with the chopped-off head. And keep your paws off my Grisly Grub Box!!! Or else . . .

Miss Battle-Axe, you are my worst teacher ever. I leave you a broken pencil.

Aunt Ruby, you can have the lime green cardigan back that you gave me for Christmas.

Hmmm. So far he wasn't doing so well giving away any of his good things.

Ralph, you can have my Goo-Shooter, but ONLY if you give me your football and your bike and your computer game Slime Ghouls.

That was more like it. After all, why should *he* be the only one writing a will? It was certainly a lot more fun thinking about *getting* stuff from other people than giving away his own treasures.

In fact, wouldn't he be better off helping others by telling them what he wanted? Wouldn't it be awful if Rich Aunt Ruby left him some of Steve's old clothes in her will thinking that he would be delighted? Better write to her at once.

Dear Aunt Ruby
I am leeving you
Something ~~great REELY~~
~~GREAT~~ REELY
REELY GREAT in
my will, so make sure
you leeve me loads of
<u>Cash</u> in yours.
  Your favorite nephew
    Henry

Now, Steve. Henry was leaving him an old pair of holey socks. But Steve didn't have to *know* that, did he. For all Henry knew, Steve *loved* holey socks.

Dear Steve

You know your new
blue racing bike
with the silver trim?
Well when your dead
it wont be any use to you,
So please leave it to me
in your will

Your favourite cousin
Henry

P.S By the way,
no need to wait till your dead,
you can give it to me now.

Right, Mum and Dad. When they
were in the old people's home they'd
hardly need a thing. A rocking chair and
blanket each would do fine for them.

 So, how would Dad's music system look in his bedroom? And where could he put Mum's clock radio? Henry had always liked the chiming clock on their mantelpiece and the picture of the blackbird. Better go and check to see where he could put them.

Henry went into Mum and Dad's room, and grabbed an armload of stuff. He staggered to his bedroom and dumped everything on the floor, then went back for a second helping.

Stumbling and staggering under his heavy burden, Horrid Henry swayed down the hall and crashed into Dad.

'What are you doing?' said Dad, staring. 'That's mine.'

'And those
are mine,' said
Mum.

'What is going
on?' shrieked
Mum and Dad.

'I was just
checking how
all this stuff will
look in my room when you're in the old
people's home,' said Horrid Henry.

'I'm not there yet,' said Mum.

'Put everything back,' said Dad.

Horrid Henry scowled. Here he was,
just trying to think ahead, and he gets
told off.

'Well, just for that I won't leave you
any of my knights in my will,' said
Henry.

Honestly, some people were so selfish.

HORRiD HENRY AND THE TV REMOTE

Horrid Henry pushed through the front door. Perfect Peter squeezed past him and ran inside.

'Hey!' screamed Horrid Henry, dashing after him. 'Get back here, worm.'

'Noooo!' squealed Perfect Peter, running as fast as his little legs would carry him.

Henry grabbed Peter's shirt, then hurtled past him into the sitting room. Yippee! He was going to get the comfy

black chair first. Almost there, almost
there, almost . . . and then Horrid
Henry skidded on a sock and slipped.
Peter pounded past and dived onto the
comfy black chair. Panting and gasping,
he snatched the remote control. Click!

'All together now! Who's a silly Billy?'
trilled the world's most annoying goat.

'Billy!' sang out Perfect Peter.

NOOOOOOOOOOOOOO!

It had happened again. Just as Henry
was looking forward to resting his weary
bones on the comfy black chair after
another long, hard, terrible day at school
and watching *Rapper Zapper* and *Knight
Fight*, Peter had somehow managed to
nab the chair first. It was so unfair.

The rule in Henry's house was that
whoever was sitting in the comfy black
chair decided what to watch on TV.
And there was Peter, smiling and singing

along with Silly Billy, the revolting singing goat who thought he was a clown.

Henry's parents were so mean and horrible, they only had one teeny tiny telly in the whole, entire house. It was so minuscule Henry practically had to watch it using a magnifying glass. And so old you practically had to kick it to turn it on. Everyone else he knew had loads of TVs. Rude Ralph

had five ginormous ones all to himself.
At least, that's what Ralph said.

All too often there were at least two
great programmes on at the same time.
How was Henry supposed to choose
between *Mutant Max* and *Terminator
Gladiator*? If only he could watch two
TVs simultaneously, wouldn't life be
wonderful?

Even worse, Mum, Dad, and Peter
had their own smelly programmes
they wanted to watch. And not great
programmes like *Hog House* and *Gross
Out*. Oh no. Mum and Dad liked
watching . . . news. Documentaries.
Opera. Perfect Peter liked nature
programmes. And revolting baby
programmes like *Daffy and her Dancing
Daisies*. Uggghh! How did he end up
in this family? When would his real
parents, the King and Queen, come and

fetch him and take him to the palace
where he could watch whatever he
wanted all day?

When he grew
up and became
King Henry the
Horrible, he'd
have three TVs
in every room,

including the bathrooms.

But until that happy day, he was stuck
at home slugging it out with Peter. He
could spend the afternoon watching *Silly
Billy*, *Cooking Cuties*, and *Sammy the
Snail*. Or . . .

Horrid Henry pounced and snatched
the remote. CLICK!

'. . . and the black knight lowers his
visor . . .'

'Give it to me,' shrieked Peter.

'No,' said Henry.

'But I've got the chair,' wailed Peter.

'So?' said Henry, waving the clicker at him. 'If you want the remote you'll have to come and get it.'

Peter hesitated. Henry dangled the remote just out of reach.

Perfect Peter slipped off the comfy black chair and grabbed for the remote. Horrid Henry ducked, swerved and jumped onto the empty chair.

'. . . And the knights are advancing towards one another, lances poised . . .'

'MUUUUMMMM!' squealed Peter. 'Henry snatched the remote!'

'Did not!'

'Did too.'

'Did not, wibble pants.'

'Don't call me wibble pants,' cried Peter.

'Okay, pongy poo poo,' said Henry.

'Don't call me pongy poo poo,' shrieked Peter.

'Okay, wibble bibble,' said Horrid Henry.

'MUUUUUMMM!' wailed Peter. 'Henry's calling me names!'

'Henry! Stop being horrid,' shouted Mum.

'I'm just trying to watch TV in peace!' screamed Henry. 'Peter's annoying me.'

'Henry's annoying *me*,' whined Peter. 'He pushed me off the chair.'

'Liar,' said Henry. 'You fell off.'

'MUUUUMMMMMM!' screamed Peter.

Mum ran in, and grabbed the remote. Click! The screen went black.

'I've had it with you boys fighting over the TV,' shouted Mum. 'No TV for the rest of the day.'

What?

Huh?

'But . . . but . . .' said Perfect Peter.

'But . . . but . . .' said Horrid Henry.

'No buts,' said Mum.

'It's not fair!' wailed Henry and Peter.

✱

Horrid Henry paced up and down his room, whacking his teddy, Mr Kill, on the bedpost every time he walked past.

WHACK!

WHACK!

WHACK!

He had to find a way to make sure he watched the programmes *he* wanted to watch. He just had to. He'd have to get up at the crack of dawn. There was no other way.

Unless . . .

Unless . . .

And then Horrid Henry had a brilliant, spectacular idea. What an idiot he'd been. All those months he'd missed his fantastic shows . . . Well, never ever again.

*

Sneak.

   Sneak.

      Sneak.

It was the middle of the night. Horrid Henry crept down the stairs as quietly as he could and tiptoed into the sitting room, shutting the door behind him. There was the TV, grumbling in the corner. 'Why is no one watching me?' moaned the telly. 'C'mon, Henry.'

But for once Henry didn't listen. He had something much more important to do.

He crept to the comfy black chair and fumbled in the dark. Now, where was the remote? Aha! There it was. As usual, it had fallen between the seat cushion and the armrest. Henry grabbed it. Quick as a flash, he switched the TV over to the channel for *Rapper Zapper*, *Talent Tigers* and *Hog House*. Then he tiptoed to the toy cupboard and hid the remote control deep inside a bucket of multi-coloured bricks that no one had played with for years.

92

Tee hee, thought Horrid Henry.

Why should he have to get up to grab the comfy black chair hours before his programmes started when he could have a lovely lie-in, saunter downstairs whenever he felt like it, and be master of the TV? Whoever was sitting in the chair could be in charge of the telly all they wanted. But without the TV remote, no one would be watching anything.

✳

Perfect Peter stretched out on the comfy black chair. Hurrah. Serve Henry right for being so mean to him. Peter had got downstairs first. Now he could watch what *he* wanted all morning.

Peter reached for the remote control.
It wasn't on the armrest. It wasn't on
the headrest. Had it slipped between the
armrest and the cushion? No. He felt
round the back. No. He looked under
the chair. Nothing. He looked behind
the chair. Where was it?

Horrid Henry strolled into the sitting
room. Peter clutched tightly onto the
armrests in case Henry tried to push him
off.

'I got the comfy black chair first,' said Peter.

'Okay,' said Horrid Henry, sitting down on the sofa. 'So let's watch something.'

Peter looked at Henry suspiciously.

'Where's the remote?' said Peter.

'I dunno,' said Horrid Henry. 'Where did you put it?'

'I didn't put it anywhere,' said Peter.

'You had it last,' said Henry.

'No I didn't,' said Peter.

'Did,' said Henry.

'Didn't,' said Peter.

Perfect Peter sat on the comfy black chair. Horrid Henry sat on the sofa.

'Have you seen it anywhere?' said Peter.

'No,' said Henry. 'You'll just have to look for it, won't you?'

Peter eyed Henry warily.

'I'm waiting,' said Horrid Henry.

Perfect Peter didn't know what to do. If he got up from the chair to look for the remote Henry would jump into it and there was no way Henry would decide to watch *Cooking Cuties*, even though today they were showing how to make your own muesli.

On the other hand, there wasn't much point sitting in the chair if he didn't have the remote.

Henry sat.

Peter sat.

'You know, Peter, you can turn on the TV without the remote,' said Henry casually.

Peter brightened. 'You can?'

'Sure," said Henry. 'You just press that big black button on the left."

Peter stared suspiciously at the button. Henry must think he was an idiot. He

could see Henry's plan from miles away.
The moment Peter left the comfy black
chair Henry would jump on it.

'You press it,' said Peter.

'Okay," said Henry agreeably. He
sauntered to the telly and pressed the
'on' button.

BOOM! CRASH! WALLOP!

'Des-troy! Des-troy!' bellowed Mutant
Max.

'Go Mutants!' shouted Horrid Henry,
bouncing up and down.

Perfect Peter sat frozen in the chair.

'But I want to watch *Sing-along with Susie!*' wailed Peter. 'She's teaching a song about raindrops and roses.'

'So find the remote,' said Horrid Henry.

'I can't,' said Peter.

'Tough,' said Horrid Henry. 'Pulverize! Destroy! Destroy!'

Tee hee.

✱

What a fantastic day, sighed Horrid Henry happily. He'd watched every single one of *his* best programmes and Peter hadn't watched a single one of *his*. And now *Hog House* was on. Could life get any better?

Dad staggered into the sitting room. 'Ahh, a little relaxation in front of the telly,' sighed Dad. 'Henry, turn off that horrible programme. I want to watch the news.'

'Shhh!' said Horrid Henry. How dare
Dad interrupt him?

'Henry . . .' said Dad.

'I can't,' said Horrid Henry. 'No
remote.'

'What do you mean, no remote?' said
Dad.

'It's gone,' said Henry.

'What do you mean, gone?' said
Mum.

'Henry lost it,' said Peter.

'Didn't,' snapped Henry.

'Did,' said Peter.

'DIDN'T!' bellowed Henry. 'Now be
quiet, I'm trying to watch.'

Mum marched over to the telly and
switched it off.

'The TV stays off until the remote is
found,' said Mum.

'But I didn't lose it!' wailed Peter.

'Neither did I,' said Horrid Henry.

This wasn't a lie, as he *hadn't* lost it.

Rats. Maybe it was time for the TV remote to make a miraculous return . . .

Sneak.

Sneak.

Sneak.

Mum and Dad were in the kitchen. Perfect Peter was practising his cello.

Horrid Henry crept to the toy cupboard and opened it.

The bucket of bricks had gone.

Huh?

Henry searched frantically in the cupboard, hurling out jigsaw puzzles, board games, and half-empty paint bottles. The bricks were definitely gone.

Yikes. Horrid Henry felt a chill down his spine. He was dead. He was doomed.

Unless Mum had moved the bricks

somewhere. Of course. Phew. He
wasn't dead yet.

Mum walked into the sitting room.

'Mum,' said Henry casually, 'I wanted
to build a castle with those old bricks
but when I went to get them from the
cupboard they'd gone.'

Mum stared at him. 'You haven't
played with those bricks in years, Henry.
I had a good clear out of all the baby toys
today and gave them to the charity shop.'

Charity shop? Charity shop? That
meant the remote was gone for good.

He would be in trouble. Big big trouble. He was doomed . . . NOT!

Without the clicker, the TV would be useless. Mum and Dad would *have* to buy a new one. Yes! A bigger, better fantastic one with twenty-five surround-sound speakers and a mega-whopper 10-foot super-sized screen!

'You know, Mum, we wouldn't have any arguments if we all had our *own* TVs,' said Henry. Yes! In fact, if he had two in his bedroom, and a third one

spare in case one of them ever broke, he'd never argue about the telly again.

Mum sighed. 'Just find the remote,' she said.

'It must be here somewhere.'

'But our TV is so old,' said Henry.

'It's fine,' said Dad.

'It's horrible,' said Henry.

'We'll see,' said Mum.

New TV here I come, thought Horrid Henry happily.

Mum sat down on the sofa and opened her book.

Dad sat down on the sofa and opened his book.

Peter sat down on the sofa and opened his book.

'You know,' said Mum, 'it's lovely and peaceful without the telly.'

'Yes,' said Dad.

'No squabbling,' said Mum.

'No screaming,' said Dad.

'Loads of time to read good books,' said Mum.

They smiled at each other.

'I think we should be a telly-free home from now on,' said Dad.

'Me too,' said Mum.

'That's a great idea,' said Perfect Peter. 'More time to do homework.'

'What??" screamed Horrid Henry. He thought his heart would stop. No TV? No TV? 'NOOOOOOOOOOOO! NOOOOOOOOOOO! NOOOOOOOOOOO!'

✱

BANG! ZAP! KER-POW!

'Go mutants!' yelped Horrid Henry,

bouncing up and down in the comfy
black chair.

Mum and Dad had resisted buying
a new telly for two long hard horrible
weeks. Finally they'd given in. Of
course they hadn't bought a big mega-
whopper super-duper telly. Oh no.
They'd bought the teeniest, tiniest,
titchiest telly they could.

Still. It was a *bit* bigger than the old
one. And the remote could always go
missing again . . .

105

HORRID HENRY'S GRUMP CARD

'I've been so good!' shrieked Horrid Henry. 'Why can't I have a grump card?'

'You have not been good,' said Mum.

'You've been awful,' said Dad.

'No I haven't,' said Henry.

Mum sighed. 'Just today you pinched Peter and called him names. You pushed him off the comfy black chair. You screamed. You wouldn't eat your sprouts. You—'

'Aside from *that*,' said Horrid Henry. 'I've been *so* good. I deserve a grump card.'

'Henry,' said Dad. 'You know we only give grump cards for *exceptionally* good behaviour.'

'But I never get one!' howled Henry.

Mum and Dad looked at each other.

'And why do you think that is?' said Mum.

'Because you're mean and unfair and the worst parents in the world!' screamed Horrid Henry.

What other reason could there be?

A grump card was precious beyond gold and silver and rubies and diamonds. If Mum or Dad thought you'd behaved totally brilliantly above and beyond the call of duty they gave you a grump card. A grump card meant that you could erase any future punishment. A grump card was a glittering, golden, get-out-of-jail-free ticket.

Horrid Henry had never had a grump

card. Just think, if he had even one . . .
if Dad was in the middle of telling him
off, or banning him from the computer
for a week, all Henry had to do was
hand him a grump card, and, like
magic, the telling off would end, the
punishment would be erased, and Henry
would be back on the computer zapping
baddies.

Horrid Henry
longed for a
grump card. But
how could he
ever get one?

Even Peter, who was always perfect,
only had seven. And he'd never even
used a single one. What a waste. What a
total waste.

Imagine what he could do if he had
a grump card . . . He could scoff every
sweet and biscuit and treat in the house.

He could forget all about homework and watch telly instead. And best of all, if Dad ever tried to ban him from the computer, or Mum shouted that he'd lost his pocket money for a month, all Henry had to do was produce the magic card.

What bliss.

What heaven.

What joy.

But *how* could Henry get a grump card? How? How?

Could he behave totally brilliantly above and beyond the call of duty? Horrid Henry considered. Nah. That was impossible. He'd once spent a whole day being perfect, and even then had ended up being sent to his room.

So how else to get a grump card?

Steal one? Hmmm. Tempting. Very tempting. He could sneak into Peter's room, snatch a grump card or two, then sneak out again. He could even substitute a fake grump card at the bottom in case Peter noticed his stash was smaller. But then Peter would be sure to tell on him when Henry  produced the golden ticket to freedom, and Mum and Dad would be so cross they'd probably *double* his punishment and ban him from the computer for life.

 Or, he could kidnap Fluff Puff, Peter's favourite plastic sheep, and hold him for ransom. Yes! And then when Peter had ransomed him back,

111

Henry could steal him again. And again.
Until all Peter's grump cards were his.
Yes! He was brilliant. He was a genius.
Why had he never thought of this
before?

Except . . . if Peter told on him, Henry
had a horrible feeling that he would get
into trouble. Big big trouble that not
even a grump card could get him out of.

Time to think again. Could he swap
something for one? What did Henry
have that Peter wanted? Comics? No.
Crisps? No. Killer Boy Rats CDs?
No way.

Henry sighed. Maybe he could *buy*
one from Peter. Unfortunately, Horrid
Henry never had any money. Whatever
pitiful pocket money he ever had always
seemed to vanish through his fingers.
Besides, who'd want to give that wormy
worm a penny?

Better yet, could Henry *trick* Peter
into giving him one? Yeah! They could
play a great game called *Learn to Share*.
Henry could tell Peter to give him half
his grump cards as Peter needed to learn
to stop being such a selfish hog. It *could*
work . . .

There was a snuffling sound, like a pig
rustling for truffles, and Perfect Peter
stuck his head round the door.

'What are you doing, Henry?' asked
Peter.

'None of your business, worm,' said
Horrid Henry.

'Want to play with me?' said Peter.

'No,' said Henry. Peter was always
nagging Henry to play with him. But
when Henry *had* played Robot and Mad
Professor with him, for some reason
Peter hadn't enjoyed giving Henry all his
sweets and money and doing all Henry's
chores for him.

'We could play checkers . . . or
Scrabble?' said Peter.

'N-O spells no,' said Henry. 'Now get
out of—' Horrid Henry paused. Wait a
minute. Wait a minute . . .

'How much will you pay me?' said
Horrid Henry.

Perfect Peter stared at Henry.

'Pay you? *Pay* you to play with me?'

114

'Yeah,' said Henry.

Perfect Peter considered.

'How much?' said Peter slowly.

'One pound a minute,' said Henry.

'One pound a minute!' said Peter.

'It's a good offer, toad,' said Henry.

'No it isn't,' said Peter.

'What, you think it should be two pounds a minute?' said Henry. 'Okay.'

'I'm going to tell on you,' said Peter.

'Tell what, worm? That I made you a perfectly good offer? No one's forcing you.'

Perfect Peter paused. Henry was right. He could just say no.

'Or . . .' said Horrid Henry. 'You could pay me in grump cards.'

'Grump cards?' said Peter.

'After all, you have tons and you never use them,' said Henry. 'You could spare one or two or four and never notice . . . and you'll refill your stash in no time.'

It was true that he didn't really need his grump cards, thought Peter. And it would be so nice to play a game . . .

'Okay,' said Peter.

YES! thought Horrid Henry. What a genius he was.

'I charge one grump card a minute.'

'No,' said Peter. 'Grump cards are valuable.'

Horrid Henry sighed.

'Tell you what, because I'm such a nice brother, I will play you a game of Scra . . . Scrab . . .' Horrid Henry could barely bring himself to even say the

word *Scrabble* . . . 'for two grump cards.
And a game of checkers for two more.'

'And a soft toy tea party?' said Peter.

Did anyone suffer as much as Henry?

He sighed, loudly.

'Okay,' said Horrid Henry. 'But that'll
cost you three.'

✱

Horrid Henry stared happily at his seven
glorious grump cards. He'd done it! He
was free to do anything he wanted. He
would be king for ever.

Why wait?

Horrid Henry skipped downstairs, went straight to the sweet jar, and took a huge handful of sweets.

'Put those back, Henry,' said Mum. 'You know sweet day is Saturday.'

'Don't care,' said Henry. 'I want sweets now and I'm having them now.' Shoving the huge handful into his mouth, he reached into the jar for more.

'Henry!' screamed Mum. 'Put those back. That's it. No sweets for a week. Now go straight—'

Horrid Henry whipped out a grump card and handed it to Mum.

Mum gasped. Her jaw dropped.

'Where . . . when . . . did you get a grump card?'

Henry shrugged. 'I got it 'cause I was so good.'

Mum stared at him. Dad must have given him one. How amazing.

Henry strolled into the sitting room. Time for *Terminator Gladiator*!

Dad was sitting on the sofa watching the boring news. Well, not for long. Horrid Henry grabbed the clicker and switched channels.

'Hey,' said Dad. 'I was watching.'

'Tough,' said Henry. 'I'm watching what I want to watch. Go Gladiator!' he squealed.

'Don't be horrid, Henry. I'm warning you . . .'

Horrid Henry stuck out his tongue at Dad. 'Buzz off, baldie.'

119

Dad gasped.

'That's it, Henry. No computer games
for a week. Now go straight—'

Dad stared at the grump card which
Henry waved at him. Henry? A grump
card? Mum must have given him one.
But how? When?

'I'll just go off now and play on the
computer,' said Henry, smirking.

Tee hee. The look on Dad's face. And
what fun to play on the computer, after
he'd been banned from it! That was well
worth a grump card. After all, he had
plenty.

Horrid Henry spat his sprouts onto the floor. But a grump card took care of the 'no TV for the rest of the day' punishment. Then he flicked peas at Peter and nicked four of his chips. That was well worth a grump card, too, thought Horrid Henry, to get his pocket money back. Bit of a shame that he had to give two grump cards to lift the ban on going to Ralph's sleepover, but, hey, that's what grump cards were for, right?

✳

'Henry, it's my turn to play on the computer,' said Peter.

'Tough,' said Horrid Henry, zapping and blasting.

'I'm going to tell on you,' said Peter.

'Go ahead,' said Henry. 'See if I care.'

'You're going to get into big, big trouble,' said Peter.

'Go away, wormy worm toady pants poopsicle,' said Henry. 'You're annoying me.'

'Mum! Henry just called me a wormy worm toady pants poopsicle!' shrieked Peter.

'Henry! Stop calling your brother names,' said Mum.

'I didn't,' shouted Henry.

'He did too!' howled Peter.

'Shut up, Ugg-face!' snarled Henry.

'Mum! Henry just called me Ugg-face!'

'That's it,' said Mum. 'Henry! Go to your room. No computer for a—'

Horrid Henry handed over another grump card.

'Henry. Where did you get these?' said Mum.

'I was given them for being good,' said Horrid Henry. That wasn't a lie, because

he *had* been good by playing with Peter, and Peter had given them to him.

Perfect Peter burst into tears.

'Henry tricked me,' said Peter. 'He took my grump cards.'

'Didn't.'

'Did.'

'We made a deal, you wibble-face nappy!' shrieked Henry, and attacked. He was a bulldozer flattening a wriggling worm . . .

'AAARRRGGGHH!' screamed Peter.

'You horrid boy,' said Mum. 'No pocket money for a week. No TV for a week. No computer for a week. No sweets for a week. Go to your room!'

Whoa, grump card to the rescue. Thank goodness he'd saved one for emergencies.

What? Huh?

Horrid Henry felt frantically inside his pockets. He looked on the floor. He checked his pockets again. And again.

There were no grump cards left.

What had he done? Had he just
blown all his grump cards in an hour?
His precious, precious grump cards?
The grump cards he'd never, ever get
again?

NOOOOOOOOO!!!!!!!

HORRID HENRY'S
BOREDOM BUSTERS

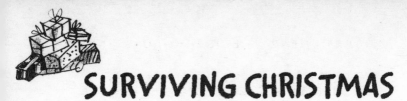

SURVIVING CHRISTMAS

THE RULES:

- Getting is better than giving – don't put too much effort into buying presents for everybody else.

- Remember to smile nicely at your parents and say 'pleeeeease' when asking for Christmas presents. If that doesn't work, scream and shout 'I hate you!'

- Sneak downstairs on Christmas Eve and hide any presents you don't want. Satsumas? NO THANKS!

- When annoying relatives visit, hide in your room with your music on full blast.

- If you don't get the part you deserve in the school play, trick the leading actor into leaving the show. Then offer to replace him.

- And when it comes to writing boring thank you letters, make sure your handwriting is as big as possible so it fills more space. Easy!

Henry

128

THANK YOU LETTER TO AUNT RUBY

Henry has written a coded thank you letter to Rich Aunt Ruby. Can you translate it?

129

TOP SECRET JOKES

Some of Horrid Henry's jokes are so rude,
he has to write the answers in top secret
code. Can you understand what he has
written?

What did the constipated
mathematician do?
Tuo ti dekrow dna licnepa tog eh.

If you're American when you go
into the toilet and American when
you come out of the toilet, what
are you when you're in the toilet?
NaeporuE.

What jumps out from behind
a snowdrift and shows you
his bottom?
Namwons elbani-mub-a eht.

Check if you're right on page 193.

✫ FESTIVE FUNNIES ✫

What kind of bread do elves
use to make sandwiches?

Shortbread.

Where is the best place to put your
Christmas tree?

Between your Christmas two and your
Christmas four.

Where do snowmen check
the weather forecast?

On the winternet.

Where did
the mistletoe
go to become
famous?

Hollywood.

How does good
King Wenceslas
like his pizza?

Deep pan,
crisp and even.

MASTERMIND

You are a contestant on *Mastermind* and your special subject is Horrid Henry. How much do you really know about him?

1. *What is the name of Horrid Henry's club?*
   a Black Hand   **b** Purple Hand
   c Green Finger

2. *Who is the other member of Horrid Henry's club?*
   a Rude Ralph   **b** Jolly Josh
   c Beefy Bert

3. *In which month is Horrid Henry's birthday?*
   a February   **b** July
   c December

4. *What is Miss Battle-Axe's first name?*
   a Boudicca   **b** Beatrice
   c Brenda

5. *Which is Horrid Henry's favourite day of the week?*
   a Monday   **b** Saturday
   c Sunday

6. *What is Horrid Henry most likely to say to Perfect Peter?*
   a Would you like to join my club?
   b Out of my way, worm
   c Let's help Mum together

7. *Is Horrid Henry's favourite band called …*
   a Happy Cannibals **b** Killer Cannibals
   c Driller Cannibals

8. *What's the name of Horrid Henry's teddy bear?*
   a Mr Cuddles
   b Mr Kill
   c Mr Grumpy

9. *What does Horrid Henry like doing best?*
   a Going on a camping holiday with his family
   b Watching TV and eating crisps
   c Going swimming

10. *Where does Horrid Henry keep his pocket money?*
   a Skeleton bank
   b Piggy bank
   c Under the mattress

Check your answers on page 193.

SCHOOL NATIVITY NIGHTMARE

Rehearsals had been going on forever. Horrid Henry spent most of his time slumping in a chair. He'd never seen such a boring play. Naturally he'd done everything he could to improve it.

'Can't I add a dance?' asked Henry.

'No,' snapped Miss Battle-Axe.

'Can't I add a teeny-weeny-little song?' Henry pleaded.

'No!' said Miss Battle-Axe.

'But how does the innkeeper *know* there's no room?' said Henry. 'I think I should—'

Miss Battle-Axe glared at him with her red eyes.

'One more word from you, Henry, and you'll change places with Linda,' snapped Miss Battle-Axe. 'Blades of grass, let's try again …'

Does Henry survive the School Nativity? Find out in 'Horrid Henry's Christmas Play' from *Horrid Henry's Cracking Christmas*.

HORRiD HENRY'S FAVOURiTE THiNGS

Horrid Henry likes his music loud,
his sweets nasty and his toys plentiful.
Can you complete five of his favourite
things by using the words below?

Terminator
Dungeon
Shooter
Killer Boy
Dirt

1. _Dirt_ Balls

2. _Killer Boy_ Rats

3. _Terminator_ Gladiator

4. Mega-whirl goo _Shooter_

5. _Dungeon_ Drink Kit

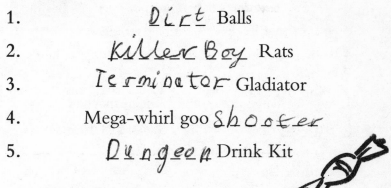

Check your answers on page 193.

135

CROSS NUMBERS

Here's a crossword with a difference –
it's all numbers! Henry is horrified!
So give him a hand with his maths
and help him fill it in.

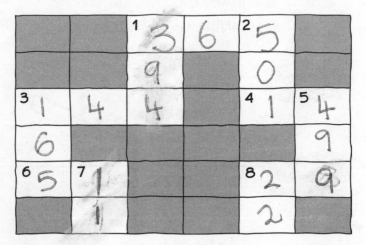

Clues

Across

1. Number of days in a year
3. 12 x 12
4. Number of days in a fortnight
6. Add 22 to 8 across
8. Number of days in February in a leap year

Down

1. 1 across plus 8 across
2. 499 + 2
3. Add 21 to 3 across
5. 501 − 2
7. Number of players in a football team
8. 7 down x 2

FESTIVE FUNNIES

Where do snowmen
go to dance?

Snowballs.

Where do ghosts go for
a Christmas treat?

The phantomime.

What's a toilet's favourite
part of Christmas lunch?

Christmas pooding.

Who delivers the cat's
Christmas presents?

Santa Paws.

Where would you find a reindeer
with no legs?

Where you left it.

CHRISTMAS GLOP

Horrid Henry and Moody Margaret
love making Christmas Glop.

You will need

A big bowl
A wooden spoon
Lots of yucky leftovers
from Christmas lunch

Instructions

1. Put the leftovers into the
   bowl and mix it all up
   into a gloppy Glop.
2. Invite your friends and
   family to a Glop tasting
   session. (Tee hee!)

HORRID HENRY'S
GLOP SURPRISE

Gravy
Brussel sprouts
Stuffing
Mashed Potato
Soup

MOODY MARGARET'S
SWEET AND SOUR

White sauce
Cranberry sauce
Mincemeat
Christmas pudding
Lemonade

GRUESOME INGREDIENTS

Forget Christmas dinner,
Horrid Henry and Moody
Margaret like making
Glop! Find some of the
ingredients they need to
make this disgusting mixture
in the wordsearch below.

COFFEE

COLESLAW

FLOUR

KETCHUP

MUSTARD

PEPPER

PORRIDGE

SEMOLINA

SPINACH

VINEGAR

YOGHURT

S	P	R	A	G	H	E	C	R	S	K
T	T	I	A	I	C	O	S	E	P	E
I	C	H	V	G	F	E	M	P	I	T
M	P	A	H	F	E	O	P	P	N	C
U	O	U	E	B	L	N	A	E	A	H
S	R	E	L	I	L	S	I	P	C	U
T	R	O	N	Q	R	I	D	V	H	P
A	I	A	C	O	L	E	S	L	A	W
R	D	P	F	L	O	U	R	Q	C	L
D	G	Z	U	D	B	G	P	A	W	R
C	E	T	R	U	H	G	O	Y	H	S

139

ARE YOU HORRID OR PERFECT?

Are you like Horrid Henry –
or more like Perfect Peter?
Do this quiz
and find out.

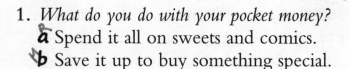

1. *What do you do with your pocket money?*
   a Spend it all on sweets and comics.
   b Save it up to buy something special.

2. *Is your bedroom . . .*
   a A smelly mess covered in sweet
   wrappers and old comics?
   b Always neat and clean?

3. *When your parents have guests round to the
   house, do you . . .*
   a Try to spoil their evening by being on
   your worst behaviour?
   b Help hand round nibbles and nod
   politely at everything they say?

4. *If you have nits . . .*
   a Do you pass them on to as many people as possible?
   b You never get nits!

5. *If the queen visited your school, would you . . .*
   a Ask her how many TVs she has?
   b Bow and say hello? You've been practising for weeks.

6. *If your parents asked you to vacuum the living room, would you...*
   a Leave the vacuum on while you watch TV?
   b Get to it right away? You need some extra pocket money for that new science book.

Mostly a's: You are a Horrid Henry! You're messy, rude, lazy and – horrid! You're always playing tricks on people and you drive your parents and your teachers crazy.

Mostly b's: You are a Perfect Peter. You're neat and nice, polite and – perfect! You love to make your mum and dad happy and you like lots of praise in return.

SANTA'S GROTTO

'What do you want for Christmas, Peter?' asked Santa.

'A dictionary!' said Peter. 'Stamps, seeds, a geometry kit, and some cello music, please.'

'No toys?'

'No thank you,' said Peter. 'I have plenty of toys already. Here's a present for you, Santa,' he added, holding out a beautifully wrapped package. 'I made it myself.'

'What a delightful young man,' said Santa. Mum beamed proudly.

'My turn now,' said Henry, pushing Peter off Santa's lap.

'And what do you want for Christmas, Henry?' asked Santa.

Henry unrolled the list.

'I want a Boom–Boom Basher and a Goo-Shooter,' said Henry.

'Well, we'll see about that,' said Santa.

'Great!' said Henry. When grown-ups said 'We'll see,' that almost always meant 'Yes'.

Does Henry get the present he asks for?
Find out in 'Horrid Henry's Christmas'
from *Horrid Henry's Cracking Christmas*.

CODE LETTERS

Horrid Henry has written a note to
Perfect Peter. He's used a secret code
so that his mum and dad won't read it
and stop him watching TV.

Can you break the code and read the note?

Clue: If A = Z and Z = A, can you work
out all the letters in between?

GROSS WORDS

Horrid Henry has made up his own crossword for you to solve. He's filled it full of the things that he hates.

Clues

Across

1. I have to go there✗ every day.

3. Soppy Snow White died ✗ after eating one of these.

4. A horrible, ✗ green vegetable.

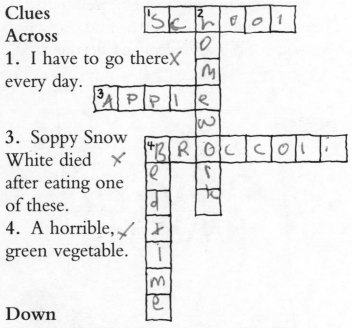

Down

2. Miss Battle-Axe makes me do this every evening. It's not fair. I want to watch TV. ✗

4. Parents always shout,"It's b̲e̲d̲t̲i̲m̲e̲" when it's still light, and there's loads of good TV to watch. ✗

BOOBY TRAP BUCKETS

Horrid Henry has set a trap for Father
Christmas to make sure he gets all the
presents he wants. Bucket A is full of cold
water, but buckets B and C are empty.
Follow the tangled strings to find out who
sets off the booby trap and gets wet.

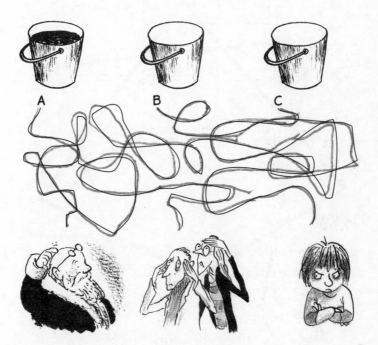

Write your answer here: A - Mum and Dad

B - Henry

C - Santa

145

CHRISTMAS STAR PUZZLE

Show a friend the star diagram below and ask them to choose a name, without telling you who it is. Tell them you are going to guess who they have chosen.

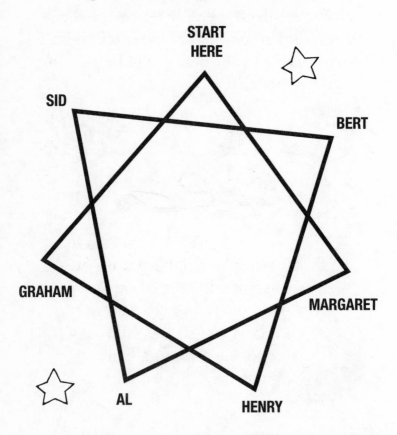

Tap the names on the star with a pencil,
asking your friend to spell the name of the
character silently, one letter for each tap.
When they reach the last letter tell them to
shout 'stop' – your pencil will be pointing
to the correct name!

Don't tell your friend, but if you
always put your pencil on the
'start here' point and tap Margaret,
Al, Sid, Bert and so on, following
the lines of the star, you'll always
guess the right name!

HENRY'S GUIDE TO STAYING UP LATE

Horrid Henry has the ultimate plan
for staying up past his bedtime on
Christmas Eve . . .

★ I take a very very very long time getting
ready for bed by brushing every tooth in my
mouth, and washing every part of my body
– at least twice. Then I ask my mum, very
politely, to iron my pyjamas because they're
a little creased. She can't complain because
she's always nagging me to be clean and
tidy, like poopy pants Perfect Peter.

★ I go downstairs for a drink of water – as many times as I dare! If my parents get annoyed, I carefully explain to them that I want to be healthy and that water is very good for me. They have to agree because they're always telling me not to drink so much Fizzywizz.

★ I turn all the clocks in the house back a couple of hours, so that my parents think it's much earlier than it really is. Tee hee!

★ If my mean, horrible parents force me to go to bed, I get up in the night and pretend to be sleepwalking. I keep my eyes open so that I don't bump into things, but I stare in a strange scary way.

If none of those things work . . .

I hide behind the sofa until everyone else has gone to bed!

Henry

HORRiD HENRY'S CHRISTMAS QUiZ

How much do you know about
Horrid Henry's Christmas?

1. *Who does Miss Battle-Axe choose to play Mary
   in the school play?*
   a Gorgeous Gurinder **b** Moody Margaret
   c Singing Soraya

2. *When Henry misbehaves, which part does Miss Battle-Axe
   threaten to give him?*
   a Hind legs of a donkey
   b Blade of grass
   c Mary

3. *Horrid Henry doesn't want a fairy on top of the Christmas
   tree. What does he want instead?*
   a Perfect Peter   **b** Mr Kill   **c** Terminator Gladiator

4. *Why does Henry set an ambush for Father Christmas?*
   a To tell him not to give Peter any presents
   b So he can rummage in his sack
   and find all the best presents
   c To tell him very firmly that satsumas are NOT presents!

5. *What did Henry give Mum and Dad for Christmas?*
   a Chocolate
   b A promise to be good for the whole of January
   c A rude poem

6. *What does Perfect Peter want for Christmas?*
a Killer Boy Rats CD
b A year's supply of Blobby Gobbers **c** A nature kit

7. *Who ALWAYS gets better Christmas presents than Henry and brags about it?*
a Beefy Bert **b** Stuck-Up Steve **c** Miss Battle-Axe

8. *What does Henry think of these presents? Match the correct answers and score one point for each:*

a Dictionary
b £15.00
c Socks
d Huge tin of chocolates
e Terminator Gladiator trident

1 Hurray!
2 Yuck!
3 OK – should have been a lot more
4 No thanks!
5 Yum

8–12 Hallelujah! You've done so brilliantly, you could have spent every Christmas with Horrid Henry!

5–7 Well done! You've got a pretty good idea of what goes on at Christmas in Horrid Henry's house.

3–4 You're obviously having such a good time at Christmas, you can't keep up with what happens at Horrid Henry's house.

1–2 Uh oh, it looks like you need to add 'Horrid Henry's Christmas Cracker' to your Christmas list!

How did you do? Check the answers on page 194.

☆ FESTIVE FUNNIES ☆

What kind of ball
doesn't bounce?

A snowball.

What does Greasy Greta put into
her Christmas pudding?

Her teeth!

What do you get if
you cross Santa
with a pirate?

Yo ho ho ho!

What do you get if you cross a bell with
nappypants Perfect Peter?

Jingle Smells!

What happened to
the thief who stole a
Christmas calendar?

He got 12 months.

What does Miss Battle-Axe
try to teach Santa's elves?

The elf-abet!

What does Santa do when
his elves are naughty?

He gives them the sack.

Stuck-Up Steve:
I want a dog for Christmas!

*Rich Aunt Ruby: Sorry darling, you're
having turkey like everyone else.*

What Christmas carol do
Horrid Henry's parents like?

Silent Night.

SNOWY SUDOKU

Fill in the sudoku so that every square
and row – both up and down –
contains these four pictures.

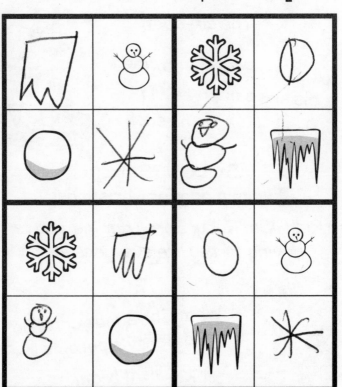

Too easy-peasy for you?
Try a trickier one! Fill in every square
and row with numbers 1-6.

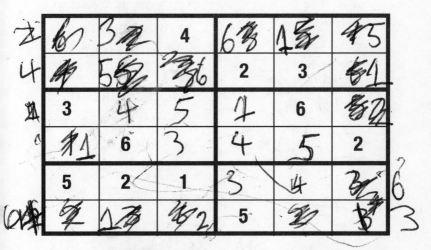

CLUE: First fill in all the missing 2's, then the 3's and 6's.

The answers are on page 195.

HORRiD HENRY'S YULETiDE RHYMES

Are you as good at writing poems as Horrid Henry? Why not have a go – Henry thinks they make great Christmas presents.

Dear Old baldy Dad
Don't be sad
Be glad
Because you've had...
A very merry Christmas
Love from your lad,
Henry

Dear Old wrinkly Mum
Don't be glum
Cause you've got a fat tum
And an even bigger bum
Love from your son,

Henry

TO THE MOODIEST MARGARET
Margaret, you old pants face
I've never seen such a nutcase
You are a stinky smelly toad
Won't I laugh when you explode

HORRID HENRY'S HORRIBLE HABITS

Horrid Henry does lots of horrible things
and some of them are listed below.
Can you find them? When you've found all
of them, the first thirteen letters left in the
wordsearch will reveal a hidden message.
Can you find it?

STOMP CHOMP DRIBBLE SHOVE KICK PINCH
~~PUSH~~ **SHOUT** ~~SLOUCH~~ ~~GULP~~ ~~SLURP~~ ~~SNATCH~~

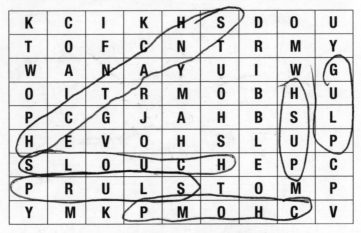

K	C	I	K	H	S	D	O	U
T	O	F	C	N	T	R	M	Y
W	A	N	A	Y	U	I	W	G
O	I	T	R	M	O	B	H	U
P	C	G	J	A	H	B	S	L
H	E	V	O	H	S	L	U	P
S	L	O	U	C	H	E	P	C
P	R	U	L	S	T	O	M	P
Y	M	K	P	M	O	H	C	V

Write Henry's message here:

<u>Out/08/my/way/worm</u>

Check if you're right on page 195.

PRESENT SCRAMBLE

Henry really wants a Dungeon Drink Kit
for Christmas, Margaret's after a
Super Soaker 2000, and Peter just wants
a new book. Follow the strings to
find out who gets what.

Henry   Peter   Margaret

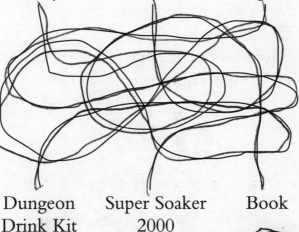

Dungeon   Super Soaker   Book
Drink Kit   2000

HORRID HENRY'S TOP TEN

The top ten presents I want for Christmas:

1. A million pounds
2. Terminator Gladiator
3. Super Soaker 2000:
   the best water blaster ever
4. Bugle Blast Boots
5. Intergalactic Samurai Gorillas
   (they launch real stinkbombs!)
6. Deluxe Dungeon Drink Kit
7. Mega-Whirl Goo Shooter
8. Day-Glo slime
9. Big box of chocolates
10. Zapatron Hip-Hop Dinosaur

Can you list your top ten?

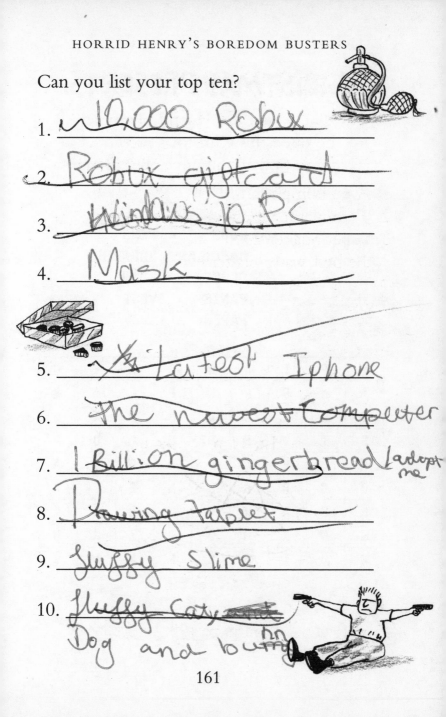

1. ~~10,000 Robux~~
2. ~~Robux giftcard~~
3. ~~Windows 10 PC~~
4. Mask
5. ~~Xt~~ Latest Iphone
6. ~~The newest Computer~~
7. 1 Billion gingerbread /adopt me
8. ~~Drawing Tablet~~
9. ~~Fluffy~~ Slime
10. ~~Fluffy Cat,~~ Dog and bunny

161

CHRISTMAS PRESENTS

"Ugh!" screams Horrid Henry as
he opens his Christmas presents.
Can you find all the unwanted presents
listed below in the wordsearch?

BOOK ✓   **PENS**

CARDIGAN ✓   **SCRABBLE**

GLOBE   **SOAP**

PANTS   **VEST**

PAPER

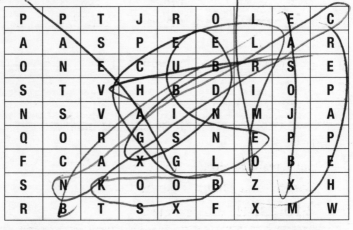

P	P	T	J	R	O	L	E	C
A	A	S	P	E	E	L	A	R
O	N	E	C	U	B	R	S	E
S	T	V	H	B	D	I	O	P
N	S	V	A	I	N	M	J	A
Q	O	R	G	S	N	E	P	P
F	C	A	X	G	L	O	B	E
S	N	K	O	O	B	Z	X	H
R	B	T	S	X	F	X	M	W

Check your answers
on page 195.

CHRISTMAS TREE CLASH

'Right, who wants to decorate the tree?' said Mum. She held out a cardboard box brimming with tinsel and gold and silver and blue baubles.

'Me!' said Henry.

'Me!' said Peter.

Horrid Henry dashed to the box and scooped up as many shiny ornaments as he could.

'I want to put on the gold baubles,' said Henry.

'I want to put on the tinsel,' said Peter.

'Keep away from my side of the tree,' hissed Henry.

'You don't have a side,' said Peter.

'Do too.'

'Do not,' said Peter.

'I want to put on the tinsel *and* the baubles,' said Henry.

'But I want to do the tinsel,' said Peter.

'Tough,' said Henry, draping Peter in tinsel.

'Muuum!' wailed Peter.

Find out if Henry gets his way in
'Horrid Henry's Christmas Presents' from
Horrid Henry's Cracking Christmas.

SPOT THE DIFFERENCE

Can you spot the four differences
between these two pictures?

1. Horse toy
2. pen
3. ornament
4. A-Z letter on book

Check your answers on page 196.

MAD MATCH-UP

You will need

20 old Christmas cards
Scissors
Two teams of players

How to play

1. Cut all the Christmas cards in half.
2. Put one batch of halves at one end of the room, and spread them out face-up on the floor.
3. Divide the remaining halves equally between the two teams.
4. Each team member in turn takes half a card, runs to the other end of the room, finds the matching piece and runs back to their team. The first team to complete all their ten cards is the winner.

HENRY'S HOW-TO-WIN TIP

When you divide out the cards, sneak the enemy team an extra card.

DINNER DISASTER

It was dark when Henry's family finally sat down to Christmas lunch. Henry's tummy was rumbling so loudly with hunger he thought the walls would cave in. Henry and Peter made a dash to grab the seat against the wall, furthest from the kitchen.

'Get off!' shouted Henry.

'It's my turn to sit here,' wailed Peter.

'Mine!'

'Mine!'

Slap!

Slap!

'WAAAAAA AAAAAAAAA!' screeched Henry.

'WAAAAAA AAAAAAAAA!' wailed Peter.

'Quiet!' screamed Dad.

Find out whether Henry ever gets to eat in 'Horrid Henry's Christmas Lunch' from *Horrid Henry's Cracking Christmas*.

FESTIVE FEAST

Find the words in the wordsearch.
The first five left-over letters spell out
Henry's ideal Christmas lunch.

S	S	P	B	I	Z	Y	Z	S	A
A	U	T	R	A	E	K	T	P	P
U	X	T	U	K	C	U	L	R	O
S	H	Y	R	F	N	O	G	O	T
A	K	U	F	T	F	R	N	U	A
G	T	Z	S	A	A	I	B	T	T
E	V	E	R	V	T	Z	N	S	O
S	H	J	Y	P	P	P	G	G	E
C	S	P	I	N	S	R	A	P	S
S	T	O	R	R	A	C	B	F	D

TURKEY   CARROTS   SAUSAGES

STUFFING   PARSNIPS   CHESTNUTS

GRAVY   POTATOES

SPROUTS   BACON

Henry's feast is: Pizza

168

FESTIVE FUNNIES

Why does Santa like to work in the garden?

Because he likes to hoe, hoe, hoe.

What's the world's strongest vegetable?
The muscle sprout.

Knock knock.
Who's there?
Chile.
Chile who?
Chile being an abominable snowman.

How long should an elf's legs be?

Just long enough to reach the ground.

What do snowmen sing at parties?

Freeze a jolly good fellow!

169

CLEVER CLARE'S CHRISTMAS QUIZ

1. *Postmen in Victorian England were sometimes called 'robins' because:*
a Their uniforms were red
b Their noses were red
c Their hair was red

2. *The little sausages wrapped in bacon that we eat at Christmas lunch are called:*
a Sausages in bed
b Pigs in a blanket
c Pigs' trotters

3. *The first sort of Christmas pudding was like porridge and it was called:*
a Frumenty
b Glop
c Ready Brek

4. *When should you take down your Christmas decorations?*
a Never – just leave your mum and dad to do it
b 24th December
c 6th January

5. *Nowadays mince pies are filled with:*
a Raisins and sultanas
b Minced beef
c Peanut butter and jelly

6. *Why is Boxing Day so called?*
a A big boxing match was always
held on that day
b It was the day for sharing the
Christmas Box with the poor
c Little brothers and sisters should
be put into a box for the day

Check out the answers on page 196.
What's your score?

Clever Clare says:

0-2 You're clueless about Christmas!
Just like Horrid Henry, I bet you think it's all
about presents.

3-4 You're quite clued-up, but maybe your
brain is ready for a long rest over the
Christmas holidays.

5-6 Happy Christmas! You're almost as
clever as me!

MERRY MYSTERY

Henry's been sent a present in the post, but he doesn't know what it is. Cross out all of the letters that appear more than two times on Horrid Henry's present. Then rearrange the nine letters that are left to find out what's inside.

Write your answer here: S̶t̶i̶n̶k̶b̶o̶m̶b̶ KIT

ROTTEN RELATIVES

Ding Dong. It must be Rich Aunt Ruby and his horrible cousin. Henry watched as his aunt staggered in carrying boxes and boxes of presents which she dropped under the brightly-lit tree. Most of them, no doubt, for Stuck-up Steve.

'I wish we weren't here,' moaned Stuck-up Steve. 'Our house is so much nicer.'

'Shh,' said Rich Aunt Ruby. She went off with Henry's parents.

Stuck-up Steve looked down at Henry.

'Bet I'll get loads more presents than you,' he said.

'Bet you won't,' said Henry, trying to sound convinced.

'It's not what you get it's the thought that counts,' said Perfect Peter.

'*I'm* getting a Boom-Boom Basher *and* a Goo-Shooter,' said Stuck-up Steve.

'So am I,' said Henry.

What does Horrid Henry get for Christmas?
Find out in 'Horrid Henry's Christmas' from
Horrid Henry's Cracking Christmas.

HORRID HENRY NAMES

Horrid Henry calls Perfect Peter lots
of rude names. Can you work out
what these six muddled-up names are?

Write your answers here

1. LYGU *ugly*

2. ATDO *Toad*

3. RWMO *Worm*

4. YLMESL *smelly*

5. PYPNA *Nappy* FACE

6. OPO *poo* BREATH

Make sure you check your answers on
page 196.

TRiCKY TRiANGLES

Miss Battle-Axe has given Henry's class some homework to do over the Christmas holidays. Boring! Can you help Henry out?

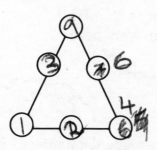

In the first puzzle, you have to move the numbers on to the rings, so that the total numbers on all three sides of the triangle equals 9.

Numbers:
1, 2, 3, 4, 5, 6

Why not try another? This time, all the sides have to equal 10.

Numbers:
1, 2, 3, 4, 5, 6

The answers are on page 196.

CHRISTMAS PARTY PROP GAME

This game is perfect for livening up
all those boring visits to your rotten relatives
over the Christmas holidays!

You will need

Tray or small table
Collection of props –
these can be anything from around the house

(Here are a few suggestions)

Newspaper   Present
Torch   Magnifying glass
Umbrella   Walking stick
Santa hat   Coat
Handbag   Book
Dog lead   Briefcase

Instructions

1. One of the players is the director and the other players get into teams.
2. The first team leaves the room, then the director chooses three of the props and puts them on the tray or table.
4. The team come back into the room and looks at the props.
5. They have two minutes to prepare a short play which must involve all three of the props.
6. Then they have two minutes to perform their play to the other team or teams.
7. The other teams do the same thing and at the end, there's a vote and the best team gets a prize. The director has the final decision!

PRIZED POSSESSIONS

Start from the grey box, then move up or down or sideways, but not diagonally, to find a winding track that includes some of Henry's prized possessions.

At the end, you'll find a toy that Henry definitely doesn't want!

1. **WHOOPEE CUSHION**

2. **SUPERSOAKER 2000**

3. **MR KILL**

4. **GOO SHOOTER**

5. **BOOM BOOM BASHER**

6. **STINKBOMB**

7. **DUNGEON DRINK KIT**

8. **GRISLY GRUB BOX**

START

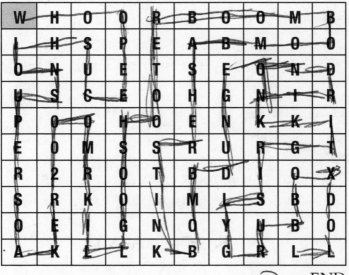

The unwanted toy is a ~~Pet~~ Doll

179

BEST GUEST LIST

Instead of having stinky old relatives round for Christmas lunch, Henry's come up with his ultimate best guest list of everyone he'd like to spend the day with instead.

Mutant Max

Marvin the Maniac

Terminator Troll

Killer Boy Rats

Can you name five amazing guests you'd like to invite for lunch?

1. RO.BLOX
2. MI NOSANG
3. EPIC GAMES
4. My friend my friend
5. Spiderman

180

PLEASE, FATHER CHRISTMAS!

Horrid Henry lay on the sofa with his fingers in his ears, double-checking his choices from the Toy Heaven catalogue. Big red 'X's' appeared on every page, to help you-know-who remember all the toys he absolutely had to have. Oh please, let everything he wanted leap from its pages and into Santa's sack.

After all, what could be better than looking at a huge, glittering sack of presents on Christmas morning, and knowing that they were all for you?

Oh please let this be the year when he finally got everything he wanted!

Does Henry get everything he wants?
Find out in 'Horrid Henry's Ambush' from
Horrid Henry's Cracking Christmas.

HORRID HENRY'S GREAT GIFTS

It's NEVER better to give than to receive. Spending hard-earned cash on presents for undeserving people is the worst part about Christmas. Remember, it's the thought that counts. And thoughts don't count.

If you don't fancy writing some poems for your nearest and dearest, how about these amazing gifts instead?

Certificates

Sweet wrapper collage

Portraits

A plastic bag (very useful)

Henry
Henry
Henry
Henry
Henry
Henry

Drawings of yourself

Your autograph

⭐ FESTIVE FUNNIES ⭐

What is Tarzan's favourite Christmas song?

Jungle bells.

Why can't you tell a joke when ice skating?

Because the ice might crack up.

Why did the turkey cross the road?

It was the chicken's day off.

What do you call a snowman on a sunny day?

A puddle.

What is Father Christmas's wife called?

Mary Christmas.

What do snowmen wear on their heads?

Ice caps.

TOP TOYS

Horrid Henry, Perfect Peter and Stuck-Up Steve are each given a different amount of money from their relatives for Christmas. They spend it on different toys. Work out who is given which amount of money, and what he buys with it. Fill in the grid.

MONEY: £12.00, £13.00, £15.00
TOYS: Globe, Dungeon Drink Kit, Day-Glo Slime

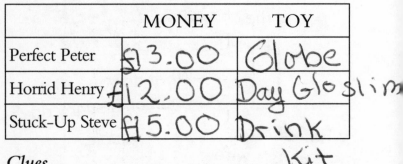

	MONEY	TOY
Perfect Peter	£13.00	Globe
Horrid Henry	£12.00	Day Glo Slime
Stuck-Up Steve	£15.00	Drink Kit

Clues

1. Horrid Henry gets less pocket money than Stuck-Up Steve and Perfect Peter.
2. The Dungeon Drink Kit costs £15.00.
3. Perfect Peter buys the toy globe.

CHRISTMAS DAY DASH

It's Christmas morning and Henry is waiting to rush downstairs and see what Father Christmas has left him (hopefully NOT satsumas!). Can you guide him through the maze to his pile of presents?

Check your route on page 197.

TURKEY TIME!

It's finally time for Christmas lunch.
But can you spot five differences between
the two pictures below?

1.

~~Paper crown~~

2.

~~Paper crown is~~ diff
color

3.

~~Mum has no~~ glass

4.

The glass is half
empty.

5.

~~Fork~~
~~knife~~ is gone

Check out the
answers on page
198 to see if you
spotted them all.

HOW TO AVOID SPROUTS

Bleuccchh! Sprouts are the WORST thing about Christmas. Follow Henry's tips to avoid having to eat them at all.

1. Convince your Mum that your brother or sister LOVES spouts so that they get double helpings. That means there'll be fewer on your plate to get rid of!
2. Sit next to someone with really bad eyesight, preferably your grandma. She'll never notice you slide your sprouts on to her plate.
3. Feed them to the dog.
4. Or the cat.
5. Hide them in the nearest draw or cupboard.
6. Flick them at your brother or sister. It's not your fault they're not quick enough to catch them.
7. Offer to help clear everyone's plates away. Your parents will be so thrilled at your helpfulness that they won't notice you quickly empty your sprouts into the bin.

187

PUNCHLINE PUZZLE

Christmas crackers should always have a joke inside. Follow the instructions below and cross out the letters in the box. Then read the leftover letters from left to right to find the answer to this cracking joke:

HOW DO YOU GREET A THREE-HEADED REINDEER?

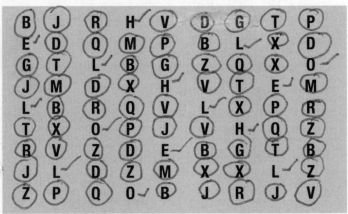

Cross-out instructions

Cross out 7 **B**'s   Cross out 6 **D**'s   Cross out 4 **G**'s
Cross out 6 **J**'s   Cross out 4 **M**'s   Cross out 5 **P**'s
Cross out 5 **Q**'s   Cross out 5 **R**'s   Cross out 5 **T**'s
Cross out 6 **V**'s   Cross out 7 **X**'s   Cross out 6 **Z**'s

Answer: H̶E̶L̶L̶O̶ , H̶E̶L̶L̶O̶ , H̶E̶L̶L̶O̶

Check out the answer on page 198.

Merry Christmas
from Horrid Henry!

Goodbye, gang!
Hope you have a really
horrid Christmas!

ANSWERS

p129 Henry's note says:
Dear Aunt Ruby, I do not like my present. Next year, don't send me underpants, a book, or socks. Send money. Henry.

p130
What did the constipated mathematician do?
He got a pencil and worked it out.

If you're American when you go into the toilet and American when you come out of the toilet, what are you when you're in the toilet?
European

What jumps out from behind a snowdrift and shows you his bottom?
The a–bum–inable snowman.

p132–133

1. *b*	4. *a*	7. *b*	10. *a*
2. *a*	5. *b*	8. *b*	
3. *a*	6. *b*	9. *b*	

p135
1. DIRT BALLS
2. KILLER BOY RATS
3. TERMINATOR GLADIATOR
4. MEGA-WHIRL GOO SHOOTER
5. DUNGEON DRINK KIT

p136

		3	6	5	
		9		0	
1	4	4		1	4
6					9
5	1			2	9
	1			2	

p139

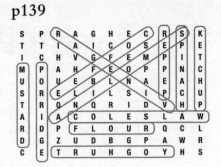

p143

Horrid Henry's note says:
PETER IS SMELLY

p144

1 across – School
2 down – Homework
3 across – Apple
4 across – Broccoli
4 down – Bedtime

p145

Ooops! Mum and Dad set off the booby trap
and get soaked. Tee hee!

p150–151

1. *b*
2. *b*
3. c
4. *b*
5. c
6. c

7. *b*
8. *a* 2.
   b 3.
   c 4.
   d 5.
   e 1.

194

p154-155

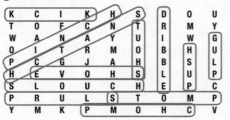

2	3	4	1	5	6
1	5	6	2	3	4
3	1	2	4	6	5
4	6	5	3	1	2
5	2	1	6	4	3
6	4	3	5	2	1

p158

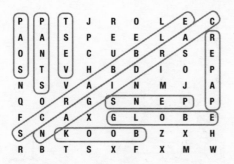

OUT / OF / MY / WAY / WORM

p159

Henry gets a book, Margaret gets a Super Soaker 2000, and Peter gets a Dungeon Drink Kit.

p162

195

p164–165

MISSING:
1. Bauble
2. Pen
3. Knight on horseback
4. A-Z lettering on book

p168

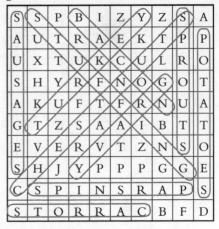

Henry's feast is: PIZZA

p170–171
1. *a*   4. *c*
2. *b*   5. *a*
3. *a*   6. *b*

p172
The mystery present is a STINKBOMB KIT

p174
1. Ugly   4. Smelly
2. Toad   5. Nappy face
3. Worm   6. Poo breath

p175

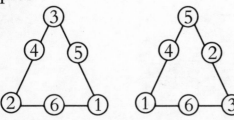

196

p178–179

START

W	H	O	O	R	B	O	O	M	B
I	H	S	P	E	A	B	M	O	O
O	N	U	E	T	S	E	O	N	D
U	S	C	E	O	H	G	N	I	R
P	O	O	H	O	E	N	K	K	I
E	O	M	S	S	R	U	R	G	T
R	2	R	O	T	B	D	I	O	X
S	R	K	O	I	M	L	S	B	D
O	E	I	G	N	O	Y	U	B	O
A	K	L	L	K	B	G	R	L	L

END

The unwanted toy is a DOLL

p184

	MONEY	TOY
Perfect Peter	£13.00	Globe
Horrid Henry	£12.00	Day-Glo Slime
Stuck-Up Steve	£15.00	Dungeon Drink Kit

p185

p186

DIFFERENCES:

1. Fork
2. Wine glass
3. Grandad's Hat
4. Mum's glasses
5. Grandma's Hat

p188
The answer is: Hello, Hello, Hello

WHERE'S HORRID HENRY

Featuring 32 pages of fiendish things to
spot, join Henry and his friends (and evilest
enemies!) on their awesome adventures –
from birthday parties and camping trips
to hiding out at a spooky haunted house.
With a challenging checklist of things to
find, this is Henry's most horrid
challenge yet!

The question is, where's Horrid Henry?

HORRID HENRY'S CANNIBAL CURSE

The final collection of four brand new
utterly horrid stories in which Horrid
Henry triumphantly reveals his guide to
perfect parents, reads an interesting book
about a really naughty girl, and
conjures up the cannibal's curse to
deal with his enemies and small,
annoying brother.

Visit Horrid Henry's website at
www.horridhenry.co.uk for competitions,
games, downloads and a monthly newsletter